Killer Cocktail

For Judy —
Enjoy!

David
Hamlin

by
David M. Hamlin

Published by Open Books

Copyright © 2021 by David M. Hamlin

Cover photo © by Christopher Lyzcen shutterstock.
com/g/CLyzcen

ISBN-13: 978-1948598460

For Sydney,
The muse who sings to me everyday

Chapter One

"First things first," said Bert Presley, WSMP-TV's News Director. "Winter, take Kern and head over to the Cook County courthouse on Washington. The Northside Women's Care Clinic is trying to get Judge Sikow to—"

"I know," said Emily. "NWCC is trying to stop an anti-abortion group from harassing their patients and the staff."

"Exactly. Right to Life Chicago has been demonstrating on the sidewalk in front of the clinic for weeks now. The clinic wants an injunction to stop them. Hearing's at the top of Sikow's calendar this morning. Likely to be some fireworks."

"Probably so, Bert. But I can't cover it."

Presley winced and gave Donald Malafronte, the station's V.P. for News & Public Affairs, a dismayed grimace.

"Really, Winter? First thing in the morning—and a damn Monday morning at that—and you're already giving me trouble?"

Emily smiled.

"Actually, I'm saving you from trouble."

"This should be good."

"No kidding, Bert. If I cover the hearing, you'll be in for a torrent of criticism."

"Because?"

"Because I've got a serious conflict of interest. ACLU is defending RTL Chicago. They're going to argue that an injunction preventing the demonstrations would be a flagrant violation of the First Amendment."

Presley glanced down at the City News Service budget, a rundown of newsworthy events for the day.

"Says here Greg Good, ACLU's Legal Director, is representing the demonstrators. How is that a conflict?"

"Good is on the papers," said Emily, "but one of their volunteer attorneys will be arguing the case."

"So?"

"The lawyer before Judge Sikow will be Benjamin Winter."

"Your Ben?"

Emily grinned.

"My Ben."

"Damn. The story's front page in both papers this morning. We figure it's this evening's lead. I wanted you on it."

"And I'd love to be there, Bert, but it's just too—"

"I got it, Winter. You're right. It's out of the question." Presley paused and a sly grin appeared for just a moment. "And here I thought you were part of the team."

The word "team" elicited a reaction from everybody in the room. A couple of producers laughed, some reporters grimaced and others rolled their eyes; Jon Stamp, who wrote copy for the evening news anchors, let out an exaggerated groan. Donald Malafronte gave an enthusiastic thumbs-up.

"Team" was the subject of considerable derision—and Malafronte's pride—in the halls of WSMP-TV, Channel 8 in Chicago. A month earlier, the station had revved up its local programming and aired several news "specials" to elevate their ratings during the critical May sweeps, one of three periods when audiences are measured; the resulting data dictated ad rates.

To drive their numbers up and their ad rates higher, the station's Marketing Department had come up with a new tag line. Everyone in the news department—anchors, reporters, the sports crew, even Billy Hutchins, the station's enormously popular weatherman—had been directed to use "Team 8" at the close of every report. At the same time, radio ads and billboards all over Chicago had announced that "WSMP's Team 8 News works for you. We're all Team8s!"

To the dismay of most, including Emily Winter, the tag hadn't vanished when the May sweep ended. They were now in early June and the Marketing Department—which was, in fact, one kid with an MBA whose office and loyalty lay in the middle of the advertising sales operation at the station—so loved the new moniker that it stayed in place. Of those in the conference room for the morning news planning session, only Daniel Malafronte truly liked Team 8, a fact Emily chalked up to the fact that he'd risen to his position after a long stint in sales.

As the snickers and smirks quieted, Presley stared at the wall above Emily's head for a moment.

"Okay. Stone, you go down to the studio and grab a camera guy, head over to the courthouse. I want good tape from this, interviews, a good intro, strong wrap, the whole schmear.

"Winter, you take Kern to the NWCC building, talk to somebody senior on the staff, maybe a patient or two, get their reactions to the demonstrations."

"I'll get demonstrators, too," said Emily.

"Of course. Stone, you should probably get going now—hearing's scheduled for the top of the hour."

"I'll leave now, too," said Emily.

"No need," said Presley, "but I know you love these meetings as much as I love having you in them—which isn't always a lot—so go ahead. It'll lower my stress level."

He gave her a wry smile.

Emily chuckled, gathered her notebook and pens and took her WSMP-TV blazer—with a Team 8 logo embroidered on the lapel—from the back of her chair.

"Bert, you mind if I give Nikki some advice, help her with the story?"

Presley shrugged.

"You'll do it anyway, right?"

"Right."

In the hall, Emily leaned against the wall while Nikki Stone set her briefcase aside and put on her blazer. Stone was new to the WSMP staff; she'd come to the station after a couple of years as a general assignment reporter in Santa Barbara. She'd been in Chicago for less than a month.

"So, Nikki, a couple of things. When you get there, check out the other reporters and find a woman, a little over five feet tall, brunette hair cut short with super tight curls. She'll probably have a pencil somewhere in the curls. When you find her, introduce yourself and tell her I said you should look her up. You have any questions, you get confused, something happens you don't understand, don't think twice—ask her for help. She knows the territory and she's a good woman."

"What's her name?"

"Lois Lipton. She'll have an ID badge—she's with the *Tribune*."

"Thanks," said Nikki. "I admit I'm a little nervous."

"Shake it off. You wouldn't be here if Presley didn't think you've got chops and he knows his stuff. Plus, there's a handful of us breaking into boy's club newsrooms and we all take care of each other—Lois is one of us and she'll be happy to help. You'll be fine."

"Thank you," said Nikki, the tension in her jaw relaxing a little. She turned to leave, then turned back.

"Did you say 'a couple' of things?"

Emily's eyes twinkled.

"Yes. When the hearing ends—no matter who wins or loses—everybody will go straight to whomever is speaking for the two groups. You need to get NWCC on tape, but skip the RTLC spokesperson and get Ben instead."

"Why?"

"You want to stand out, bring back something which gives our audience a fresh perspective."

"I don't understand."

"All the others will probably talk to the RTLC leaders, so if you interview my husband, you'll stand out from the crowd."

Stone frowned.

"But if everybody else is—"

Emily held up a hand.

"Everybody else won't know what you know," she said.

"I don't get it."

"What you know is this, Nikki—Ben Winter is deeply devoted to free speech and he gets positively eloquent about it. It will take him a moment or two to work up to it, but if you're patient and keep the tape rolling, you'll get great, informative, passionate stuff. Trust me—you want to file something that sings, right?

"Okay," said Stone, but there was anxiety in her eyes.

"Listen, Nikki, this is more than just another story, it's tonight's lead. You file something strong,

Bert will notice and you'll go from being the new kid to being one of us. I've been where you are, fighting to make it, to break through. You want to make an impression, let 'em know you're as good as the guys. Use Ben. Trust me."

With Scott Kern at the wheel, Emily rode north on Lake Shore Drive in one of the station's news cars, an enormous Plymouth station wagon. They exited at Belmont and headed west to Clark Street, then north past shops and restaurants and grocery stores until they arrived at the double-wide storefront which housed the Northside Women's Care Center.

There were two large frosted windows on the front of the building, but the only signage was painted on the entrance door, small lettering which said "NWCC: Ring bell for admittance." Emily pushed the button and a voice crackled through a box above the door.

"How can we help you?"

"Emily Winter, WSMP news. I'm with Scott Kern, my cameraman. We'd like to talk to Carmen Howorth, please."

"Right. Wait there."

They stood on the sidewalk. Emily scanned the area and turned to Kern.

"No demonstrators," she said.

"I noticed. Think they're all at the courthouse?"

"Probably. Too bad, that. I would have given them

plenty of time to explain their mission. Bert's going to be annoyed, they aren't here. Let's hope Stone gets some tape we can fold in."

"Yup."

"I'll buzz you in now," said the box.

When the buzzer sounded, Kern turned and backed in, holding his bulky camera away from the door frame. Emily followed him. They entered a narrow hallway. Two arrow signs hung from the ceiling; the one pointing to the door on the right said "Reception & Intake;" the one pointing left said "Clinic Patients and Staff Only."

The receptionist behind the desk rose to greet them. There were two women sitting in the lobby. One of them saw Kern's camera and Emily's blazer and jumped up, walking past them and out the door; the other remained in her seat but she raised the magazine she was reading high enough to hide her face.

"Is this about the lawsuit?"

"Yes," said Emily. "We'd like Ms. Howorth—she is the Executive Director, isn't she?—to give us some background."

"She's on the phone right now with somebody from the *Sun-Times*. She'll see you when she's done."

Emily frowned. It wasn't realistic to hope for an exclusive—she knew the lawsuit was too hot for that—but she was still disappointed that somebody had beaten her to Howorth.

"Okay," she said, "we'll wait. Okay if we sit?"

The receptionist glanced at the woman hiding

behind her magazine.

"Yes, but please don't bother our clients."

Emily nodded, but she was conflicted. She recognized, and was prepared to honor, the privacy of the women who used the clinic, but she also had a story to cover. To do it justice, she'd need to find out how women who had run the gauntlet of demonstrators had reacted to it, had felt about it. She decided that an interview with the clinic's director was most critical and elected to forgo clients, but only for the time being. She settled into the plastic chair most removed from the woman behind the magazine while Kern leaned against the wall next to Emily, his camera and tripod on the floor between his feet.

Twenty minutes later, the receptionist told them Ms. Howorth was ready.

"Go through that door," she said, "to the administrative office. It's just one big room. Carmen's desk is back in the corner."

There were six desks in the room. Each displayed a nameplate featuring the NWCC logo, a name and a title. There were desks for a business manager and two fundraisers and one which said "Patient Support Services." In the back corners, one desk said Carmen Howorth, Executive Director, the other Joan Estrada, MD, Clinical Director.

Howorth was a tall brunette with short hair and bright blue glasses. She rose to meet them, smiling broadly and bending over to shake Emily's hand.

"I'm guessing you want to know about our suit,"

she said.

"Indirectly," said Emily. "We've got a reporter downtown covering the hearing. I'm here to get some background and add a more personal perspective to our coverage."

Scott Kern set up the tripod and fixed his camera to it. He checked the angle and the focus and then attached a small rectangular light to the top of the camera.

"Boy, that's bright," said Howorth. "Should I do something with my makeup?"

"What do you think, Scott?"

He checked his view again.

"Nah. She looks great. The white blouse is a little hot, though."

He adjusted the angle of the light.

"Good," he said. "Ready when you are, Emily."

Emily pointed her hand-held mic at Ms. Howorth.

"First, if you would, say and spell your name for us. Then, tell me about the impact these demonstrations are having on your clinic."

Howorth gave her name and Emily held up one hand for a second or two, getting Howorth to pause, and then nodded. Later, she'd edit out the name and start after the gap; the ID would appear on a chyron below her image.

"The women who come to us for healthcare are often vulnerable. Some aren't well—we get a lot of UTIs—"

Emily pulled the mic back.

"Our audience may not know what that means."

"Of course. Sorry, inside jargon," said Howorth. "We get a lot of urinary tract infections, expectant moms who want to be sure their pregnancies are proceeding as they should or need pre-natal care, many seeking birth control counselling. We go out of our way to make them comfortable but, as you can imagine, most of our patients are anxious. When they are met with jeers and anger and derision before they even come through the door, it only adds to their stress."

"What do they hear?"

"The demonstrators call them names—I won't repeat them, but they aren't pleasant. Many tell us they've been accused of murder even if they aren't pregnant. They hear some pretty cruel stuff. They get yelled at and taunted and the signs they see are cruel, too. 'Abortion is murder,' 'Dead babies are a sin,' 'God will punish you,' that sort of thing."

"Have you lost any patients?"

Howorth frowned.

"That may be the worst part. We don't know how many women in need of care give up and leave to avoid the anger they'll face, but we do know that the number of visits per week has dropped since the demonstrators started showing up; we're down by about thirty percent. We hope they're finding help somewhere else, but of course we can't know that. We understand that many people have strong feelings about the care we provide, but that shouldn't prevent women from getting the care they need."

"You do perform abortions here, right?"

"It's true that we terminate first term pregnancies as a last resort, but we provide a lot of guidance and support before we do that. We talk about adoption, we explain how babies find a home through a surrogacy agreement, we explain all the risks involved and we make every effort to alert them to the emotional impact a termination can have. It's ultimately the woman's choice—and we're adamant that it is her choice alone—but it's not like they walk in and get the procedure instantly. We take terminations very seriously."

"That's what I need," Emily said. "Is there anything else you'd care to add?"

"People should understand that the demonstrators inflict emotional harm on women who don't deserve it. Our staff—on the administrative side and the clinical side, where our nurses and Dr. Estrada work—feel like they're working in a war zone. They're frightened to come to work but they come to work anyhow because our patients need them. When those who disagree with our mission prevent us from serving that mission, they are doing far more harm than good."

Howorth's delivery was sincere and emotional. Emily smiled and nodded.

"You're very good at this," she said.

"Thank you."

"Got what you need, Emily?"

"Yes, thanks, Scott."

Kern switched off the camera and its bright light.

"Ms. Howorth—"

"Please, call me Carmen."

"Okay. Carmen, I'd like to talk to one or two of your staff and some of the women you care for. Is there a way to arrange that?"

"The staff part is easy. As you can see, it's just me and the receptionist here today. Everybody else is in the field or at the courthouse. Our medical staff have the morning off because Joan is at the hearing too; there's just one nurse to cover emergencies. But tomorrow, I can make one or two of them available to you.

"Our policy is to protect our clients' privacy at all costs, so I can't just turn you loose in the lobby or give you contact information. What I will do is ask Sharon Sanderson, she's our in-house counsellor, a trained psychologist, to find one or two patients she thinks would be willing to talk about the care they get here. She'll get their permission before you talk to them, of course. They may all say no. you understand."

"I do. I'll check with my boss, but I think we can interview them without exposing them—no names, no faces—if that helps."

"It might. Let me chat with Sharon about that."

"Here's my card," said Emily. "Have her contact me directly."

"Okay."

The phone on Howorth's desk buzzed and she picked it up, listening for a second.

"I'm sorry, but this is a call I have to take. Can you find your way out?"

"Yes," said Emily. "Thanks again—you've been very helpful."

Kern stowed his gear and Emily led him back toward the lobby. At the door, she turned and took a few steps back toward Howorth's desk.

"Thanks for what you do," she said. "It's good to know you're here to care for us."

Howorth, her phone cradled on her shoulder, waved and smiled.

Chapter Two

"Let's get right to it," said Judge Jonah Sikow. "Who's here?"

"Good morning, your Honor. I'm Elizabeth Proctor on behalf of the Northside Women's Care Clinic."

"Good day, sir. I'm Benjamin Winter for ACLU representing Right to Life Chicago."

Ben executed a modest bow.

"Okay, then. Miss Proctor, you've filed a petition seeking an injunction?"

"Exactly, your Honor. NWCC has been the object of protests and the demonstrators are harassing our patients and staff, disturbing the peace and impeding our ability to conduct our business."

"Which is abortions, right?"

"No, your Honor. While we do perform terminations, our care focuses primarily on women's health issues in general."

"Like I said, abortions."

"Those procedures account for roughly twelve percent of our—"

Sikow rapped his gavel.

"I get the picture, Miss Proctor. Mr. Winter?"

"Your Honor, the demonstrators have absolute, inviolate rights to freedom of speech and assembly. The injunction plaintiffs seek would be a clear violation of those rights. The First Amendment governs this circumstance, the more so since there is no doubt that our client is engaged in political speech, speech which courts have protected without reservation since the Bill of Rights came into being."

"Hold on. Is ACLU here representing an anti-abortion organization?"

"Yes, your Honor."

"But, ACLU supports abortion, right?"

"We support women's right to privacy, yes, but we also support everyone's right to free speech, your Honor. ACLU has a long tradition of protecting the rights of those whose views we may or may not endorse."

"Probably gonna cost you fellas some donations, Mr. Winter."

"I'm a volunteer, sir, but I have full faith and confidence that ACLU understands the risks. Financial peril will not dissuade us from defending this important principle."

"Oh, right. That Voltaire fellow, wasn't it? 'I disagree with what you say but I'll defend your right to say it'. Something like that."

"With respect, your Honor, Voltaire never said that. It is typically attributed to him, but in fact it was a biographer who used the phrase to describe

Voltaire's view. The thought is apt, however."

"I want to know stuff like that, Mr. Winter, I'll head down to Champagne-Urbana, take a course. You can shut up, now," said the judge.

Then, under his breath, "Smart ass."

A side door behind the judge's bench flew open with enough force to bang against the wall. Everyone, including the judge, turned to see a clerk with a slip of paper in his hand dash toward the judge's desk.

"I apologize for the interruption, your Honor," said the clerk, "but the deputy chief is on the line. He says it's urgent that he speak with you."

"Dan Mallory?"

"Yes, sir. He says he has information pertinent to this case for you."

"We'll be in recess."

Sikow rose and moved to the back door apace, his robe billowing behind him. There was a moment of silence and then a buzz emerged. Elizabeth Proctor leaned over to the woman at the table with her and talked quietly. A sizable number of RTLC supporters, sitting behind the railing, began chattering in whispers. Ben Winter had a quiet discussion with the man and woman seated at the defense table with him.

In the row of seats where the press had assembled, Nikki Stone turned to Lois Lipton.

"What's going on?"

"I have no idea," said Lipton. "Pretty unusual to cut off the hearing and take a call. If I had to guess, I'd imagine that Mallory has something to say about the demonstrations. Chicago police have been called out several times since the demonstrations began. Maybe CPD brass knows something. We'll just have to wait and see."

Several minutes later, Judge Sikow returned to the bench. The room rose and then sat when he resumed his seat.

"Mr. Winter. Is there someone here representing your client?"

"Yes, your Honor. Our witnesses include the co-chairs of the organization and a number of RTLC members."

"I want to hear from the head honcho."

"Your Honor—"

"Be quiet, Mr. Winter. I want somebody on the stand. Now."

Ben turned to the two people at his side. The two whispered and the man rose.

"Your Honor, Norman Brent will speak for my client."

"Get up here, Mr. Brent."

Brent, a heavy-set man in rumpled slacks and a Hawaiian shirt, snaked his way past the defense table. The clerk swore him in and he took the witness stand to Judge Sikow's right.

"For the record, sir, state your name and position."

"My name is Norman Brent. I am Co-Chair of Right To Life Chicago."

"You responsible for these demonstrations at the clinic?"

"I help coordinate them, but a lot of people are involved."

"Have you been part of the action?"

Brent sat up tall and looked directly at Sikow.

"We've been protecting precious life for nearly a month now, your Honor. I haven't missed a demonstration yet—I've been to all of them."

There was overt pride in his statement.

"Well, then, sir, tell me this. Are your demonstrators waving signs at people driving by?"

"Some carry signs. Yes."

"And that causes traffic to slow down. Clark Street's pretty busy in that neighborhood, isn't it? People in cars slow down to yell at you, right?"

"Mostly they just honk."

"And these people with signs, do they step off the curb?"

"I don't understand."

"It's a simple question, sir. Do your people get in the way of traffic?"

"Well, no, not really. There's street parking, so there are usually parked cars between us and the traffic."

"Not the way I hear it. Let me ask you this. Do you people prevent anyone from going into the building?"

"No, sir."

"You don't stop them, maybe yell at them a little? Maybe call them names, call 'em 'killers?'"

"Your Honor, I object." Ben Winter rose from his chair. "The First Amendment and a voluminous bank of case law are perfectly clear, sir. In the U.S., we do not censor speech based on its content and certainly not in a political context such as this one. My client's beliefs are not and cannot be on trial."

"Overruled."

Sikow turned to Norman Brent.

"You all shout at these women? You accuse them of crimes?"

"Your Honor, a sidebar, please."

Sikow glared at Winter for a long moment.

"No reason to drag this out, Mr. Winter."

"I appreciate that, your Honor, but—"

"Approach the bench. Be quick about it. You, too, Mrs. Proctor."

"It's Ms. Proctor, your Honor."

"Whatever. Get up here."

Benjamin lowered his voice; Sikow muffled his microphone with a meaty hand.

"Your Honor, it appears that the call you just took has had an impact on your view of this case."

"I work with our cops, Winter. We need to protect our city."

"I appreciate that, you honor. Still, if Deputy Chief Mallory has, in effect, testified on the matter before this court, I assert the defense's right to cross-examine him. We have the right to confront our accusers."

"You got anything to say about this, Mrs. Proctor?"

Proctor flinched at the repetition of Mrs., but she shook her head.

"Back to your tables, then."

"Your Honor," said Ben.

"Winter, I'm only going to say this once. You'd be smart to pay attention. Drop this or I'll find you in contempt and you can enjoy a visit to our holding cell down in the basement."

Ben drew a deep breath.

"For the record, your Honor. We object."

Sikow turned to his stenographer.

"Let the record reflect that Mr. Winter here has registered his objection. Let it also reflect that this court is governed by my rules, not his. Back to your seats. Now."

Sikow turned back to Brent.

"So, you shout at these women or not?"

"We believe all life is sacrosanct, your Honor. We share that view with women who may not respect the right to life of the unborn."

"Women on the street? Women on their way into this clinic? You share your views with them?"

"Of course, your Honor. That's why we're there."

"Not for long. Take a seat."

Sikow turned to the plaintiff's table.

"Mrs. Proctor, do you have a draft of the injunction you wish to impose?"

"We have, your Honor."

"Hand it over."

Proctor moved around her table and presented a single piece of paper to the clerk who handed it to the judge. He glanced at it and pulled out a pen.

"Looks good to me."

Ben Winter rose.

"Your Honor, if I may—"

"What?"

"Before you sign that, your Honor, my client wishes to be heard on the First Amendment implications of an injunction. Of equal importance, sir, there may be viable options which enable the court to accomplish its goals without subjecting your Honor's decision to review in higher courts."

"You telling me you'll appeal?"

"Without question, your Honor. If the injunction plaintiffs seek is executed, we'll file an emergency appeal before lunch today."

Sikow scowled, but there was a hint of apprehension behind it.

"If I may, I wish to suggest a more efficient approach, your Honor, one which will save the parties—and your Honor—the cost and time an appeal will necessitate. It is even possible that your Honor can fashion a plan which satisfies both sides."

Sikow's scowl disappeared.

"What do you have in mind, sir?"

"Cox versus New Hampshire, your Honor."

"What the hell is that?"

"A Supreme Court ruling, your Honor, 1941."

"Never heard of it."

"The U.S. Supreme Court held that, so long as the content of the speech is not a contributing factor, a court is free to dictate the time, place and manner of free speech and assembly."

"So?"

"So, your Honor has the authority to impose some limitations on our client's demonstrations so long as those limitations do not prevent their protected speech. My client will still enjoy their free speech rights while the clinic can continue its operations."

"I can do that?"

"The case is quite clear, your Honor."

"No kidding. Mrs. Proctor, what do you think?"

Elizabeth Proctor huddled in a whispered conversation with the woman sitting next to her.

"Your Honor, we would accept an order which protects our clients, both current and prospective, and the clinic's employees. We insist that no physical contact take place between our patients and the demonstrators. We want assurances that anyone can move freely on the sidewalk in front of our facility and have unfettered access to our entrance and that our staff be free to conduct business as usual."

"Mr. Winter?"

"A perimeter around the entrance would not violate our clients' rights, your Honor. If the demonstrations can take place on the same side of the street as the clinic, but come no closer than, say, 100 feet from the entrance, their rights will be protected and the clinic's entry will remain readily available."

"Mrs. Proctor?"

"Three hundred feet, your Honor."

Sikow pondered, his eyebrows almost touching one another.

"Two hundred fifty feet in both directions, same

side of the street, no physical contact. That satisfy you all?"

Ben turned and had a quick whispered conversation with Norman Brent and the woman beside him.

"So long as our client's right to speak and assemble is not materially impeded, we accept the court's judgment. Such a ruling would be consistent with the Cox case."

Elizabeth Proctor and the woman at her table also huddled.

"Your Honor, my client, represented here in the person of its Chief Medical Officer, Dr. Joan Estrada, will agree to those conditions. We ask that the order be preliminary, however, so it reserves our ability to come before you again if we find that the restrictions are not sufficient or if the defendant violates them."

"Done," said Sikow. "You all get together and draft it up, I'll sign it. By noon today. So ordered. That will be all."

Judge Sikow rose and the room rose with him. He turned to leave and then swiveled around.

"Winter, what's the name of that case again?"

"Cox v. New Hampshire, sir."

"Cite it in the agreement. One of you tries to take this thing above my head, I want the record to reflect that I'm issuing an order consistent with Supreme Court rulings."

Bellman

Good evening, Chicago. For Team 8, I'm Joel Bellman alongside Brent Hopkins. In our lead story tonight, a Cook

24

County Judge has issued an order which places limits on Right To Life Chicago's controversial demonstrations at the headquarters of the Northside Women's Care Clinic.

Hopkins

Our reporters have been covering this story all day today. First, here is Team 8's Nikki Stone with a report from the courtroom.

Stone

Judge Jonah Sikow issued an order this morning which requires Right To Life Chicago to remain at least 250 feet away from the entrance to Northside Women's Care Clinic. The ruling came after Judge Sikow heard testimony from RTLC's co-chair, Norman Brent. We talked with the clinic's medical director, Dr. Joan Estrada, right after the judge issued his order.

Estrada

NWCC is pleased that the court has agreed to let women seeking health care enter our facility without being subjected to harassment. The Supreme Court's ruling in Roe v. Wade *affirms every woman's right to choice when it comes to childbirth and, while we also offer a wide variety of other services to our patients, we are pleased that this ruling supports that right. NWCC's patients and our staff will be free to provide careful and considerate care to the women of Chicago.*

Stone

In a surprising twist, the American Civil Liberties Union, which has long defended the Roe versus Wade decision, appeared in court today representing Right To Life Chicago. The ACLU's volunteer lawyer, Benjamin Winter, vigorously defended the group's right to demonstrate at the clinic.

B. Winter

The First Amendment is the heart and soul of our democracy. It protects the rights of all to speak and to assemble in support of their cause. Today's ruling allows RTLC to continue to express its point of view, even if that message is delivered to those who clearly disagree with it. We are all free to express our ideas, just as we are all free to reject ideas with which we do not agree. That is precisely what the founders envisioned when they gave us the Bill of Rights and Judge Sikow's ruling correctly honors that rich and vital American tradition.

Stone

Immediately after the ruling, Right To Life Chicago's Norman Brent told Team 8 that his organization will resume demonstrating near the clinic immediately. For Team 8, I'm Nikki Stone.

Bellman

Team 8 also spoke with Carmen Howorth, NWCC's Executive Director. For that side of the story, here's Team 8's Emily Solomon Winter. Emily. . .

E. Winter

There was no demonstration today at the Northside Women's Care Clinic, although there have been demonstrations here for a month and the clinic expects that RTLC will resume their vigil again tomorrow. We asked NWCC's

Carmen Howorth to explain why the organization asked the court to halt the demonstrations.

Howorth

People should understand that the demonstrators inflict emotional harm on women who don't deserve it. Our staff—on the administrative side and the clinical side, where our nurses and Dr. Estrada work—feel like they're working in a war zone. They're frightened to come to work but they come to work anyhow because our patients need them. When those who disagree with our mission prevent us from serving that mission, they are doing far more harm than good.

E. Winter

Since RTLC plans to continue demonstrating at this Clinic and the clinic has no plans to curtail its services or close its doors, we can expect that this controversy will not go away any time soon. WSMP will continue to monitor the situation for developments. For Team 8, I'm Emily Solomon Winter.

Bellman

In other news today, former Miss America Anita Bryant's Save Our Children crusade secured a victory when Dade County in Florida repealed an ordinance which banned discrimination on the basis of sexual orientation. To explain that vote and the controversy surrounding Miss Bryant's efforts in Florida, Brent will discuss the issue with Team 8's legal expert, Stephen Spellman. Brent. . .

Chapter Three

"What's this?"

Emily Winter walked into the condominium on the first floor of the building on Inner Lake Shore Drive and nearly tripped on a wicker basket in the entryway.

Ben Winter came out of the kitchen wearing an apron; he had a roll of tin foil in one hand.

"Good evening, m'love. You see before you the essential requirement for dining al fresco, a picnic hamper: cold chicken, potato salad, coleslaw, a bottle of wine, chilled, two plastic glasses, two plastic forks, paper plates and napkins. Some cubed cheddar and sliced apple to start us off and your favorite, chocolate chunk cookies, for dessert. They just came out of the oven."

"We're having a picnic? And you baked?"

"We are indeed. The weather is ideal—warm enough to sit on a blanket in the park, relatively low humidity, a soft breeze off the lake. You'll want to change, I think, into something which will keep you cozy when the sun is fully down. That blazer is fashionable, but I suspect your colleagues would be upset were it to display grass stains.

"I've encased the cookies in a double layer of foil, so they may still be warm when we're ready for them."

"You, sir, are a wonder."

"And you, ma'am, are the best part of any picnic. Go change. I can get the portable radio out so we can have music with our repast."

"Nope. I'd much rather talk."

"As would I, m'love. As would I."

Emily changed into jeans and threw on a sweatshirt which was at least two sizes too large. Ben carried the hamper and Emily took his free arm, a red blanket draped over her shoulder. They took the elevator from the first floor down to the lobby, exited and strolled across the Inner Drive. They walked across the park and found a spot where the waning sun wasn't blocked by their building or the ones nearby and settled down.

"So," said Emily with a small smile, "You were in the news today."

"I was. The print people chatted me up after the hearing. It was interesting to see Ms. Lipton at work. She was by far the most informed of those working the story. And I did a brief interview with one of the TV reporters, too."

"Nikki Stone."

"The very same. She was the only one from TV who interviewed me. I don't suppose you had a hand in that?"

Emily laughed. "Guilty as charged, sir. I knew you'd be eloquent, as usual, and I wanted Nikki to bring back something the others wouldn't. It worked, too—we're the only station which used a clip from you. And you were as good as I knew you'd be. Very sharp."

"Although not perfectly bespoke," said Ben. "I watched the early newscast. My tie was askew."

"I saw the raw footage when we edited Nikki's piece and mine for broadcast and I didn't notice that. I doubt anyone did."

"I did."

"Of course. You would. But you were on point and very clear and concise. That's what matters, right?"

"In the long run, yes. Could you tell I was somewhat restrained? Judge Sikow is a pompous hack and he's something of a martinet. I was tempted, sorely tempted, to chide him for taking testimony from the police *in camera*. A travesty, testimony behind closed doors without cross-examination. And of course, there's the glaring fact that he was, how shall I put this? He was ill-prepared."

"I didn't think you were holding back. He wasn't prepared?"

"The fellow knew it was a First Amendment case, speech and assembly, but he hadn't done a lick of homework. A dedicated jurist would have done a modicum of research at the least. Even the most cursory search would have led him to the Cox case and thus to 'time, place and manner.' Sloppy work, but I suppose one can expect little more from a judge whose primary qualification is years of dedicated service as a ward heeler."

"But you led him to the right decision."

"I cannot say, for sure, whether it was my argument or his desire to avoid being reviewed by a higher court—I'm told he is the most over-turned judge in the municipal system—but it did come 'round right in the end. And your day, m'love?"

"Well, I was disappointed that none of the demonstrators were outside the clinic. I wanted their point of view to be heard. Bert did, too, although he wasn't cranky about it. I thought Scott and I got good material from Howorth."

"She made her case quite well," said Ben.

"Yes, she did. She's dedicated to the clinic and it was obvious when she spoke, so it was good on the air. But, right after we wrapped up with her, I did something which worries me a little."

"What?"

"When we were done, I stepped over the line, Ben. I broke the wall. I thanked her for the work she does."

"And you find that worrisome? Why?"

"It wasn't objective. I'm supposed to be a neutral observer, not a participant. I shared my own views with her. It wasn't appropriate."

"Rather too strict, I think. There was no indication of your personal views when you did the interview. You maintained your objectivity until your job was done, did you not?"

"I suppose so, but later, after I'd praised her work, it felt like I was more of an advocate than a reporter."

"But you are an advocate. Did you not fight long and hard to bring justice for Beni Steinart when you were at WEL? Not so long ago, you wouldn't give up on the CARD murder until you found the complete story. Your passion is an asset, m'love, not an impediment."

"My champion. I love you for that, among other things, but this was not the same thing. Carmen Howorth probably thinks I'm on her side now and that's not where a reporter should be."

"Really?" Ben gave her a wide grin. "Aren't you part of the team? Doesn't WSMP work for us?"

"That's the point, isn't it? That stupid slogan implies that it's a game and we're playing in it. News isn't about picking sides, it's about delivering the facts. We should be referees, not teammates. I should have kept my mouth shut."

"After the fact, after you'd done your job? It strikes me as a trifle, Emily, of little consequence. Besides, you're hardly alone in seeking to balance one's professional responsibilities with one's personal views. It is a matter of irrefutable fact that Norman Brent is a misogynistic zealot whose view of the role of women is entirely corrupt. His co-chair, Carol Lobes, is just as bad—they seek to reduce women, all women, to chattel. I wouldn't spend two minutes with either of them under any circumstances, but I set my disgust aside to argue the law on their behalf. I see little difference. We both did our jobs, quite capably, did we not?"

"I suppose so," said Emily, "but I'm going to be more careful from now on."

"As you wish. Ready for some chicken?"

"And some more wine, please."

———————

Two weeks later, Bert Presley sent Emily to Northwestern Law School to interview a criminal justice professor for the evening's lead story. Having been convicted of conspiracy to obstruct justice and perjury, Richard Nixon's close advisor Bob Haldeman was about to serve a two and a half to eight-year sentence. Presley wanted an expert to explain the nature of the charges and illuminate the system of justice which holds one and all, even the most powerful, as equal before the law.

Emily wrapped up the segment efficiently. Scott Kern had another assignment to complete, so he took the station wagon, leaving Emily to fend for herself. She called the City Cab dispatcher and Ben's Uncle Max appeared in a hurry, his cab sparkling inside and out.

"Max Winter at your service," he said as she climbed into the front seat. "You call, I drive. Where we going?"

"Clark Street, Max, the Northside Women's Care Clinic."

"Something going on there?"

"A demonstration, I hope."

"Trouble?"

"Not as far as I know. Since Ben convinced Judge Sikow that Right To Life Chicago could continue protesting at the clinic, they've been there every day. There haven't been any incidents so far, but I'm curious to see how it's going. I'm thinking about pitching a follow-up story. I'd like to find out how both sides are coping, see if the restrictions Sikow put in place have made a difference. And I'd like to see if RTLC is obeying the injunction."

"The guys in the garage gave me the business that day, when Ben was on TV and all. They thought you used your clout so he'd get on the air."

"I did encourage our reporter to interview him, but I don't have the clout to get him on the air—those decisions are made by the suits higher up. He's good at it, so there wasn't a lot of doubt they'd use him, but I was hands-off. Sort of."

"Yeah, but I bet they listen to you. I mean, you're the chief investigative reporter over there, right? That's gotta be worth something."

"Well, I do get to go to boring meetings every morning; not sure what that's worth, and they let me do my job, but that's about it, Max. The truth is, I wasn't allowed anywhere near Ben's part of that story—it wouldn't have been right."

"They shoulda asked me," said Max. "The two of you on the tube together, same time, the family would be over the moon for weeks."

"I hate to tell you, Max, but the guys who run the shop don't actually spend much time thinking about the Winter family's gatherings. Besides, you do so much bragging about both of us, you don't need their help."

"Yeah? Well, they need mine. How they think you get around this city, no driver's license? I'm the guy gets you where you need to go, right? Come to think of it, they oughta put me on the payroll."

"Don't hold your breath, pal."

"Think about it. A limo would be too flashy, but their best reporter oughta have a car and driver, you ask me. I'm seeing a lot of them Chevy Impalas on the streets, one-a them would do the trick. Lots of room in the back, you could keep all your stuff back there, always at the ready."

"Dream on, Max. Dream on."

"Hey, a fella can hope, right? This must be the place—there's a bunch of folks with signs over there, but they aren't at the clinic. They're down the street."

"That's where they're supposed to be, Max. Pull over and let me out."

"You want me to wait? I'll tell dispatch I caught a long haul."

"Nope. I don't know how long I'll be and, besides, you're supposed to be driving paying fares, not going off the clock to take care of me."

"Aw, forget about that. I'm aces with the bosses. Got connections with all the big hotels, get more convention work than anybody else. You don't gotta worry about me. You sure you don't want me to wait? How're you getting home?"

"I'll catch a bus, Max."

"Okay, but you need me, you know where to find me."

"Yes, I do."

"Damn straight. Go get 'em."

Emily climbed out of the cab and stood on the opposite side of the street to observe. The demonstrators were honoring parts of the deal. They were well removed from the entrance to the clinic and they were being careful not to step off the sidewalk or engage any of the drivers passing by.

Two of the group were more aggressive than most. A woman with an ID badge and a black armband stood near one corner of the block; when women walked toward the clinic, she fell in step with them as they moved forward. Emily couldn't hear her, but the woman appeared to be talking—maybe whispering—to each woman she shadowed. She was careful to stop at the court-ordered boundary, but the women she engaged seemed uncomfortable; a couple of them looked visibly angry.

On the other side of the perimeter, a young man—possibly still a teen—displayed an angry demeanor, glaring at women as they passed him. He was holding a sign which Emily couldn't read; most of the women he confronted seemed annoyed and discomforted.

Emily walked to the corner and crossed the street. She stood on the corner and waited while the woman who was matching strides with others made her way back to her starting point. When she reached the corner, Emily approached her.

The woman's badge said "RTLC Carol Lobes, Co-Chair."

"Ms. Lobes, I'm Emily Winter, with WSMP-TV news. May I ask you a few questions?"

"It's *Mrs.* Lobes, young lady. I'm a happily married woman, just so you know, and proud of it."

"So am I," said Emily with a smile.

"What do you want?"

"I'm curious about your encounters here. I noticed that you're following only women, not men."

"Men don't go into the place."

"I was across the street, so I couldn't hear anything. Are you talking to them?"

"I'm not allowed to do that. I pray for their souls and recite the sixth commandment."

"Thou shalt not kill?"

"That's it. Abortion is murder. Any woman who has one is killing a baby. I believe that they will suffer an eternity of pain and anguish if they go into that place to destroy a life."

"How do you know that's what they're doing? For one thing, not all the women on this sidewalk are going to the clinic in the first place."

"A little prayer won't hurt them. And it's an abortion clinic, isn't it?"

"Most of the women who use the clinic are getting medical care, not abortions. They need a doctor. Lots of women are more comfortable with a female physician."

Carol Lobes snorted.

"So, you're on their side?"

"I'm not on anybody's side, ma'am. I'm just trying to find out how Judge Sikow's order is working."

"Really? You sound like one of them."

"I do? A majority of the women who use the clinic aren't even pregnant. That's just a fact, Ms. Lobes. I'm just telling you what I know."

"Whatever you say, dear. And it's Mrs. Lobes—don't make me tell you again."

A smartly dressed woman cut between them and Lobes fell in step with her, muttering quietly as the woman moved forward. When they reached the court-ordered perimeter, Lobes turned back. The woman kept striding, past the entrance to the clinic and down the sidewalk. When she was a few steps past the entrance, she turned and looked back at Lobes, shaking her head.

Emily walked through the open zone and approached the young man she'd noticed earlier.

His sign said: "What About The Dad?"

"Hi," said Emily, "I'm a reporter with WSMP-TV. Can I talk to you for a minute or two?"

He gave her a thorough once-over and said, "Yeah."

"Thank you. Can you explain your sign to me?"

"Isn't it obvious?"

"Not to me."

"Yeah? Well, think about it. Those women going into the place are getting abortions, right?"

"A few of them, yes."

"Well, how'd they get knocked up? It wasn't immaculate conception, right?"

"No, I suppose not."

"So, what about the dad? What if the guy wants his kid? Doesn't he have any rights?"

"I believe the law says it's the woman's right to choose, not the man's. I'm not a lawyer, but the way I understand it, the Supreme Court ruled that forcing a woman to have a child or interfering with her healthcare violates her right to privacy."

"Yeah," said the young man, "the father doesn't count."

His eyes flashed and his anger hung in the air. Emily wasn't frightened, but she did sense that it would be prudent to back down a little. She smiled and extended her hand.

"Sorry, I didn't introduce myself. I'm Emily Winter," she said.

His glare softened just a little.

"Sam Terhune."

"There's something else I'm wondering about, Sam."

"What's that?"

"You're a good deal younger than all the other people in this group. They're all grown-ups, but you're, what, seventeen, eighteen?"

"Eighteen. Just graduated from Parker."

"Congratulations. That's a fine school."

"It's okay. I'm glad to be through with it—it was hard work, that place."

"Going to college?"

"Yeah. I'll be a freshman this fall. U-Conn."

"Connecticut?"

"Yeah. It's where my girl goes. She's a year ahead of me."

Emily sensed something and an instinct loomed; she deliberated for just a moment and decided to follow it.

"Has she had an abortion?"

His eyes grew hard and he glared at her. Then, the glare vanished and his eyes turned sad and damp.

"Yeah."

"At this clinic?"

"Yeah."

"I'm sorry," she said. "Can you tell me about it?"

He sighed and looked away, gazing into the distance.

"I wanted to marry her. It would have been tough, but it was the right thing to do and I really love her. She loves me, too. It would have been a struggle for us, for sure, but we could have made it work, I know we could have.

"But her parents wouldn't stand for it. They sent her to this place and she didn't, she couldn't. . .she said she thought it was best. She said we'd have kids, but later, when we graduate and all."

"That must have been painful."

"I didn't get a vote," he said. "They didn't even

tell me when. I found out after it was over. I couldn't even be with her when it happened."

"And that's why you're here?"

"All summer, right up to the day I leave for school. I want them to think about the fathers, the men who get left out."

"A lot of men don't feel the way you do," said Emily. "A lot of men probably don't even know they've gotten somebody pregnant and I think a lot of others are happy to duck the responsibility."

"I'm not one of them," said Sam. "And the people in there"—he pointed at the clinic—"the people in there didn't care. They didn't care at all."

His gaze drifted away again, but she still felt his rage.

"I hate them," he said.

Emily wasn't certain that his hatred was directed at the clinic or the girlfriend's parents, or both, but she didn't want to press.

"I may want to talk with you again," she said. "Is there a number where I can reach you?"

"I'm at home until I leave for Storrs."

She wrote down the number and walked away.

Chapter Four

"Emily's here," said Linda Marshall, "we have a quorum, plus one. The Rules Committee is in session. Who's your guest, Emily?"

The women in the booth at Riccardo's adjusted their positions to make room for one of the new arrivals; Emily snagged a chair from an adjoining table and sat.

"Hi, gang," said Emily. "This is Nikki. She's new in town, doing general assignment work with us at 'SMP.'"

Emily took a sip of wine and extended her arm, sweeping around the table.

"Nikki Stone, this is Mary Massey, senior producer, WMAQ, Linda Marshall, business reporter on Channel 24, Abby Evans, feature writer and critic at *The Reader*. Marcy Marcus is the program director at Y98 FM, Kirsten Bonner is the Communications V.P. with Cary Chase Enterprises, Becca Bloomfield is an Account Executive at Foote Cone & Belding. You've already met Lois Lipton, from the *Trib*."

"Hi, glad you could join us," said Lipton, turning to address her colleagues. "Nikki and I covered the hearing about stopping the demonstrations at NWCC. She filed a good piece."

Nikki blushed.

"Thank you. Truth is, I'm still finding the bathrooms."

"Time was, there weren't any," said Marshall. "When some of us broke through, we had to leave the office, walk down the hall, take an elevator just to pee."

"Second that," said Emily. "When I was on the overnight beat at the cop shop, the bathroom was so disgusting I didn't want to use it even when they let me. I still have creepy dreams about that pigsty. Even after they accepted me—to the extent they did—that place was definitely a men's room."

Lois turned to Nikki. "We've all been the first woman and it can be brutal. That's pretty much how we came together, finding our way. We had no idea what the rules were, so we kind of drifted into this weekly gathering."

"We eventually figured out that there aren't any rules," said Mary Massey, "or at least there aren't any worth following, but we still get together to try to sort it out."

"And drink," said Bloomfield, "drinking helps."

"Hi, Nikki. We meet every Friday night," said Bonner. "May I gently suggest that when Emily's glass gets empty, you buy her the next one?"

"I'd be happy to," said Stone, "is that one of the rules?"

"Nope. Remember, there aren't any rules. But, it

will serve to acknowledge that without Emily, you probably wouldn't have your job. There used to be a glass ceiling at 'SMP. Women only did soft features or weekend weather until Emily broke through."

"I'm hardly the only one," said Emily. "We've all left shards of glass on the floor."

Massey grinned.

"True, but that won't stop you from accepting a free drink, will it?"

"Nope," said Emily.

They talked, laughed and drank, carrying on a boisterous, occasionally bawdy conversation which ranged across acres of topics. They discussed current events, office gossip; they had a spirited discussion about whether *Laverne and Shirley* was a feminist show or not. They reached an overwhelming consensus that John Travolta was one handsome fellow but his TV show was dumb.

After some ninety minutes, Ben came into the bar and found their table. He had just enough time to greet the women before their close friends Greg and Alicia Good arrived; Emily made her farewells and the two couples left for dinner.

Greg Good suggested, with considerable conviction, that they dine at Berghoff. Everyone agreed, so they hailed a cab and, to Greg's delight, secured a table without a wait.

When they were seated, Greg Good said, "Thanks for indulging me. I've been aching to have good Wiener schnitzel for at least a week and this place has it in spades."

"One good reason to support the choice," said Ben. "I offer another. They make their own root beer."

"Drinks are on me," said Good.

Ben frowned.

"Don't be absurd, pal. We'll split the check."

"No, I insist."

"And I refuse."

Emily and Alicia exchanged a look.

"Knock it off, boys," said Alicia.

"We're not on the playground," said Emily.

Ben grinned. Greg signaled the waiter.

"One check," he said, "we'll split it, right?"

"Right," said Ben.

Their drinks arrived and they ordered.

"So, Ben, I know Greg is most grateful for your support on the NWCC suit," said Alicia, "but I haven't seen you since you handled that case and I want to thank you as well."

"Shucks, ma'am," said Ben, "'t'weren't nothin'. Just another skirmish."

"But an important one," said Alicia.

"When it comes to defending the First Amendment in this town," said Greg, "there's no such thing as a 'skirmish.' Official Chicago treats free speech like a rabid dog; they think the only way to deal with it is to beat it into submission."

Emily laughed.

"That won't happen while you two are on the case," she said. "But I'm curious, Alicia. Why are you thanking Ben?"

"Because Ben's solution made it easier for NWCC to do our job. I'm on NWCC's board of directors," said Alicia. "Didn't you know that?"

"I didn't. Is this new?"

"Not exactly. It's been nearly a year. They've got a couple of doctors and an accountant on the board and several members who have a lot of money. Greg and I donate, of course, although not at the level others do, but last year the attorney who'd been sitting on the board, a gal from Sidley & Austin, resigned so they asked me to take her seat."

"Good for you," said Emily. "Tell me about the funding. Isn't the clinic non-profit?"

"It is. We charge reasonable fees for service to those who can afford it, but a lot of our clients are young single women who can't afford to pay full rates. Some can't afford to pay anything at all, but Carmen and Joan are adamant that they won't turn anyone away, so there's a sliding fee scale. The board oversees governance and policy, but we spend a lot of time hustling our friends and colleagues for donations or tables at the annual dinner."

"Most commendable," said Ben.

"I met Carmen Howorth when we reported on the suit," said Emily. "I thought she was exceptionally sharp. I haven't met Joan Estrada, but Ben has. She went out of her way to thank him after the hearing. I thought that was classy."

"That's Joan. All grace and compassion," said

Alicia. "I had to go the extra mile every day in law school because they all thought women couldn't handle it—there were only four of us in that class—but from what Joan tells me, my experience was a picnic compared to what she endured in med school. She didn't just survive, she grew stronger and wiser. I really admire her."

"After the hearing, she told me the restrictions the court imposed would make it easier for women to visit the clinic," said Ben. "To be fair, she also told me that she wouldn't have been exactly heartbroken if they'd won the suit outright, but she was gracious about that, too."

"In any event," said Greg, "our Ben was at his usual better than best that day. Here's to you, Benjamin Winter. A job well done."

He lifted his glass in toast and both women joined him. Ben blushed a little and waved them off. He was relieved when their waiter and two busboys approached to serve them before he had to say anything.

"Alicia, I've been thinking about the confrontation, RTLC and your clinic. There's so much tension around *Roe v. Wade*, it's been, what, close to four years now and if anything, the abortion debate is even hotter. I think there might be a story there."

"It's not just tension," said Alicia. "There's a lot of anger on both sides and real passion, too. I think the RTLC people are dead wrong, but I admire their determination. They're true believers, just as we are."

"The two people I dealt with, Norman Brent and Carol Lobes, sure believe," said Ben. "I had to be more than circumspect when we met before the hearing and they kept talking about murder and baby killers. You're right, they are entirely devoted to their convictions."

"And I think that's a good story," said Emily. "Rock solid, unwavering positions on both sides. The demonstrations are still happening every day, so there's a natural hook. If I can persuade my boss that there's something there, Alicia, would you be willing to do an interview? I'd get staff involved, but it might be good to hear from the board, too."

"It should probably be our board chair," said Alicia, "but if she wants to pass, I'd be glad to do it."

"That's great," said Emily, "Anyone interested in dessert?"

"Me," said Alicia.

"I'll have a root beer," said Ben.

———

"I don't know, Emily," said Bert Presley. "There's nothing new here, is there? The clinic's been around for a couple of years, the right-to-life people have been screaming about legalization since before that Supreme Court case—"

"*Roe v. Wade*," said Emily.

"Yeah, that one. They've been on the warpath ever since. It's sort of like the anti-war thing, isn't it? Those people were in the streets every day, picket lines, rallies, vigils—we didn't cover that stuff unless it was huge or somebody did something big. You know, blow up a bank or throw eggs at Kissinger. Bunch of people walking up and down a sidewalk at the clinic? I don't see a hook."

"There's high energy and passion—anger, too—on both sides, Bert. It's a debate that's not going to go away. I think a deeper look—get beyond the slogans, find out what motivates the people on both sides—would make a good piece. We do it right, both sides will tune in to make sure we give them a fair shake."

"We're not in sweeps, Emily. Maybe it would work next Fall. Besides, I've got something I want you to check out."

"What?"

"Closed Circuit TV. Last time I gassed up, my usual station, there was a crew there, installing video cameras. Inside and out. I been using that station for years, it's on my way in here, so I know the guy who runs the place. I had a chat about it with him."

"How is this a story?"

"Turns out, my guy's part of a group, operates more than four dozen stations in the city and the 'burbs, and they're all installing these things. They figure it's a security measure, helps cut down on stick-ups, vandalism. At my station, they got signs all over the place, warning people they're on camera."

"I still don't see it."

"I did a little digging. I see a couple of angles.

First, this stuff's been around since the forties, mostly for military use, industrial plants, but now the price has come down a lot, so it's accessible and more and more commercial operations are using it. Insurance companies like it, too, helps them sort out claims and they've got some numbers suggesting it cuts down on crime.

"Plus, how many people you think have any idea they're on camera when they're pumping gas? Or, what? Buying a doughnut, picking up the dry cleaning. Like I say, more places are using it."

"Bert—"

"I think it's worth checking out. People don't want to be on camera, people who resent being treated like criminals. You know, 'I'm just getting a cruller here, what right do you have to take my picture?' We talk to some random customers, get their reaction, maybe check in with the cops, find a store owner who's been held up and they caught the guy 'cause they had him and his gun on TV, just like a crime show only real, it'd be great if we had the tape, right? You could talk to the company that installed these things at the gas stations, find out how much business they're doing, how many times a day somebody's gonna be on camera, like it or not. And maybe there are some lawyers out there, think it's all an invasion of privacy or maybe argue that the tape is inadmissible when some stick-up guy goes to trial."

Emily sighed.

"There's one more thing you need to know," said Presley. There was a note or resignation in his tone.

"What?"

"Don put me onto this."

"Malafronte? He's pitching stories now? I thought he was the budget and administration guy."

"He fancies himself a news guy, too," said Bert. "A week or so ago, he saw a crew at his station, doing the same thing I saw last weekend. Only reason I noticed, come down to it, was that he'd flagged it for me. He suggested the piece and I think there may be something there."

Emily had worked with Presley long enough to recognize resignation. She also knew that Malafronte—her boss's boss—carried weight and that made resistance even more futile. While she didn't find the story particularly interesting, she could see that the angles Bert had suggested might lead to a story of some interest, however modest, to the audience. She wasn't particularly keen to take the assignment, but she didn't see a way around it.

"Tell you what, Bert," she said. "Let's swap. I'll do the piece on these cameras—I'll get on it today—but at the same time, let me chase down the abortion controversy. That work?"

Presley chuckled.

"I keep hoping that someday you'll be just a little less, what? Relentless? Persistent?"

Emily laughed.

"Determined?"

"Yeah, that. Pushy works, too. Okay. Get me a good two, two-and-a-half, maybe even three-minute piece on surveillance cameras. If nothing else breaks, you can get started on your thing. Even if we don't air your stuff, we'll have good file tape banked when we need it, so make it evergreen, right? Interviews we can use months from now if we need them."

"Deal," said Emily.

"For now. But if I need you to drop it and move to something more pressing, you promise to let it slide?"

"Okay."

"Atta girl. Always the team player."

Presley grinned.

"That's me. You know I just adore being a teammate."

"Get outta here."

"Aye, aye, sir."

Chapter Five

"How did you come to be part of RTLC?"

Emily was in Carol Lobes' den, a comfortable small room in an ordinary suburban tract home in Elk Grove Village. Scott Kern had wired both women for sound and set the camera on its tripod for a stationary two-shot; he stayed with the camera so he could zoom in on one or the other as needed. He was sipping the coffee Lobes had offered; he looked a little bored.

"My church," said Lobes, with a smile. "I'm a good Catholic girl, parochial schools from kindergarten on, spent a lot of time in CYO when I was a teen, mass every Sunday. The church teaches that abortion is a sin and I wasn't raised to question the teachings. RTLC holds workshops in a lot of the parishes and when they came to ours, I volunteered."

"I understand, but I'm curious about the contradictions."

"There are no contradictions. Thou shalt not kill is crystal clear to me."

"It is unambiguous," said Emily, "but, tell me,

doesn't the church also view rape as a sin?"

"Of course."

"But, isn't it a sin to force the victim to confront the crime she's suffered every day for the rest of her life? Even if she loves the child, she still suffers the anguish of rape every day just by being a mom. That seems to favor the rapist, the sinner, over the innocent, his victim."

"The pregnancy is God's will. That baby could grow up to become a saint or a great parish priest. What if it's a girl and when she's grown up, she marries Jesus and serves the poor as a nun? Who are we to interfere with God's plan?"

"How long have you been with RTLC?"

"Oh, golly, it's been a while. Right after the Court's horrid decision, I guess. I started out stuffing envelopes and sitting at tables on sidewalks, after mass, collecting money or getting signatures on petitions. They asked me to become part of the steering committee and after a while, I was appointed as a co-chair. Norman chairs the meetings, but I supervise the volunteers and coordinate collections. I manage things like flyers and posters, too. It makes me feel like I'm serving a higher calling; I'm honored to do whatever they need."

He chairs, you do the grunt work, Emily thought, *at least their sexism is consistent.* She stifled the urge to point it out.

"Do you all raise a lot of money? Do you have a big budget?"

"We raise what we need, usually. The Lord provides. We also have an angel."

"An angel?"

"Yes. Jon Haskill. He's a very successful executive, you know, the head of his own company. He's not married and he makes a lot of money and he's one of the Church's major donors. When you came into town, did you notice the beautiful new rec center next to our church?"

"I think we drove past it. Two stories, playground, a basketball court?"

Lobes nodded, smiling.

"It's called Jon's Place," said Lobes. "There's a big gym inside, the kids use it all the time, playing basketball and things; I think CYO holds dances there, too. Our bridge club meets there, in one of the meeting rooms. Mr. Haskill didn't pay for it all by himself, but he gave so much the diocese named it for him."

"And he supports RTLC, too?"

"When we need something badly, he's always there. He paid for a new copy machine last month. I think he pays the rent on our office, too. Our committee reviews the budget every time we meet and it always shows our rent, paid in full by an anonymous donor. We all figure it's Mr. Haskill. His generosity in service of the Lord is something special. Would you like some more coffee?"

"No, thank you," said Emily.

"How about you, young man? Would you like another cup?"

Scott Kern grinned.

"Sure. Thank you. And if you happen to have another one of those delicious muffins, I wouldn't say no."

Carol Lobes blushed.

"You're such a dear," she said. "I made them myself."

Lobes rose from her seat and started to leave.

"Just a moment, ma'am," said Kern. "If I don't unplug that mic, you'll never make it to the kitchen."

"Oh, dear," she said, "I forgot it was there."

When she left, Kern stretched out an arm to show Emily his watch.

"You still planning to cover the surveillance camera installation at three o'clock?"

"I'm afraid we don't have a choice," said Emily.

"Then we got about half an hour," said Kern. "We're meeting them in Schaumberg, we gotta hit the road pretty soon."

"Okay. I'll wrap it up when she gets back."

Carol returned with a warming pot, a muffin and a large glass jar. She topped off Kern's cup and handed him the muffin and a fancy paper napkin.

"There you go," she said, "I'm so glad you like the muffins. My husband claims they're the reason he plays golf all weekend—it's the only way he can keep his weight down, he says, but I'm pretty sure he likes being on the course, too. And please open that jar—it's got peach preserves I put up last year and everyone says they're perfect on the muffin."

She laughed and Emily heard the pride in it.

"Ms. Lobes, do you happen to have a phone number for Mr. Brent? And maybe Mr. Haskill, too?"

"It's Mrs. I don't understand that Ms. thing."

"I apologize, Mrs. Lobes—you told me that when we met at the clinic and I forgot. I'm sorry."

"It's okay, dear," she said. "It just makes me a little uncomfortable, is all. Makes me feel like I'm not married and marriage is such an important part of our faith. I don't want anyone to think I don't honor my church's teachings."

"I doubt anyone would make such a mistake," said Emily. "If you'll just get me those numbers, we'll be on our way. We have another story to cover before we head back to the station."

"It must be exciting, covering all these stories every day."

"Golly gee, it sure enough is," said Kern, "it's a thrill a minute."

Emily shot him a look but he ignored it and set about breaking down his gear to pack it up.

The van in the parking lot at the MidAm gas station in Schaumburg displayed a large colorful logo—Bad Guy Eyes—on its doors and its roof. The two technicians wore starchy overalls with the same logo on their backs. One was attaching a camera to a lamp post near the pumps; the other was inside installing the third of three cameras in the ceiling.

Emily approached the man near the pumps first. He was on a ladder and looked down on her when she waved at him.

"Can I help you, babe?"

"Emily Winter, WSMP-TV News, sir. I'd like to ask you a few questions about the system you're installing here."

"News? You from the TV, honey?"

"Yes. WSMP. You know, Team 8 News."

"Yeah, I know. Don't watch it myself."

"Can I ask you—"

"You can ask all you want, sweetie. I ain't going to answer."

"There's nothing wrong here, sir. We're just interested in the use of these cameras for security and you're sort of an expert."

"I hang 'em, I turn 'em on. Don't make me no expert. Jeff, he's the guy inside, he's in charge of the wiring and the tape machines we use for storage."

"Should I talk to him, then?"

"Won't do you any good. Only ones allowed to talk to reporters about what we do are in the main office in Skokie. I talk to you, they'll fire my butt. Jeff, too. You gotta see the honchos at headquarters, darlin.'"

"When I spoke to the office earlier, the woman who answered the phone told me where you'd be working this afternoon. She didn't tell me you can't talk about your work."

"That's Margie, she's the boss' wife. Too dumb to hum, that girl. Probably doesn't know the rule about talkin' to the press, but I do. She just wasted your time, honey, 'cause there's no chance I'm talkin' to you."

"Got it. Sorry to bother you."

"No bother. Good lookin' cutie-pie like you's a lot more interesting than climbing up and down ladders and hugging gas pumps all day. You wanna hang around, this is our last one today, me 'n Jeff'll buy you a couple of drinks after."

"Oh, darn," said Emily. "I have to go back to the station and work."

She considered saying something more—pointing out his obvious sexism—but concluded that silence would be better than sarcasm or muted anger if only because either one would likely be lost on its target.

Inside the station, which sold snacks, coffee and soft drinks as well as anti-freeze, oil and other automotive essentials, Emily approached the youngster behind the counter.

"Hi," she said, "Emily Winter, WSMP-TV News."

"Sarge is in the first service bay, right through that door."

"Sarge?"

"He's the manager. You need anything, he's the guy. If you'll just step aside, I got customers waiting in line here."

"Sure."

Sarge was all but prone under the hood of a pick-up truck, one foot on the concrete and one leg pointed straight out for balance.

"Excuse me, sir."

He held his position but swiveled his head around

to look at her.

"Yeah?"

"Emily Winter, WSMP-TV News. We'd like to talk to you about the security cameras you're installing here."

"Two seconds," he said.

He used a wrench to torque a bolt down tight and carefully extracted himself. He was a hefty fellow and Emily was surprised at how gracefully he moved.

"What?"

"Can you tell me why you're installing the closed-circuit system?"

"Sure. Last three months, we been hit four times. Three of 'em shoplifters, grabbed stuff off the shelves and bolted out the door. Latest one, the guy claimed he had a gun in his pocket, held up my night clerk—all MidAms are open 24-7—got away with everything we'd taken in after I cleaned the register out at five. Probably close to two hundred bucks. Clerk was so spooked he couldn't describe the guy at all. If that camera they're putting up behind the counter had been there, the punk'd be in the slammer already."

"Could I get my camera man over here so we can record your story?"

"Nah, I don't think so."

"Are you sure? We'll take a shot of the place from the outside, people who see it will know they're a little safer if they fill up here."

"Yeah?"

"Sure. If everybody thinks the bad guys don't come around your business because they know they're going to be on TV and get caught, isn't that good for business?"

He thought it over.

"Nah. I gotta finish up this job then I got a tune-up to do before quittin' time. Plus, I look like I just took a grease shower, I'd need to clean up some to be on the TV, that'll waste time, too. I'm gonna pass."

"Too bad," said Emily.

She turned to leave, hesitated and turned back.

"Did they provide any literature before you decided to install the cameras?"

"Who?

"Bad Guy Eyes. Did they send a salesman to talk to you, maybe he left a brochure or a contract for you to look over?"

"Yeah, you got that right. Guy in a suit, talked real smooth. He left me some stuff. Not sure where I put it—wait, now I remember. You go back to the register, ask the kid behind the counter to check the drawer under the register. I think the stuff's there."

"That would be helpful. Thank you. May I keep it?"

"Yeah. They're supposed to have these gizmos all ready to go before they leave today, I don't need their sales crap anymore."

"Thank you," said Emily.

The clerk handed her the literature and she glanced at it long enough to confirm that all the contact information for the company appeared on the back page. She dropped it in her satchel and went back to the station wagon. Scott Kern was in the driver's seat, dozing and listening to a White Sox game on the radio.

"No dice," said Emily. "Let's head back."

"Roger that," said Kern.

Chapter Six

"Dr. J is at her desk. You can go right in."

Emily left the waiting room and walked through the door to the administrative side of the Northside Women's Care Clinic. Every desk in the room was empty save Joan Estrada's; the overhead lights were off and a green lampshade on the doctor's desk cast a warm patina on the area at the back of the room.

"Good morning," said Emily. "Thank you for fitting me in."

Estrada rose to greet her and Emily was surprised to see that the woman was almost exactly as tall as she.

"It's my pleasure. Carmen said your interview with her was smart and we were all pleased with the clip you used after the court case. I apologize for the early hour, but my calendar is always full most days, and that's before about a dozen things get added to it. This is the best time for me, but I know it's awfully early."

"Not for me," said Emily. "I used to get up at three thirty in the morning. I haven't had to do that in a while, but my internal clock still wakes me earlier than I'd like, so seven thirty in the morning isn't a problem."

"Three thirty in the morning? That's debilitating. I had horrendous hours like that when I was in med school and during my internship. It takes a toll, doesn't it?"

"I never quite got used to it. There were an awful lot of blurry days back then. I missed a whole lot of primetime TV, too. But I liked the job and I learned a lot. I probably wouldn't be where I am without that experience."

"We all pay our dues, don't we? Women more than men."

Emily smiled. "The guy who hired me for that job told me that it wasn't good enough for a man but it was too important for an intern so he hired a woman."

Estrada grinned. "Why do you think I'm an OB/GYN? It was what I planned to do any way, but there was no way they were going to let me into cardiology or ENT back then. Shoot, they spent most of my first year telling me I should drop out and go to nursing school instead."

"Women's work," said Emily. "When I signed on as a journalism major, they told me I'd be better off in the school of education. Do you ever wonder if we should have listened to them?"

"Not for one second."

"Me either."

"Is it true you're married to the lawyer who represented RTLC?"

"Yup, Ben's my guy. ACLU was counsel of record, but he volunteers with them on occasion. He came away with a lot of respect for you."

"I admired his work as well. We wanted to get that injunction, but he had me wondering if we'd made the right call. I was worried that he might win for their side until he told the judge about that 'time, place and manner' option. Impressive. I don't think the judge knew the first thing about that case."

"Ben didn't think so either. That injunction is part of the reason I'm here. Have the restrictions on the demonstrators helped? It's been a couple of weeks now. Have you noticed a difference?"

"Our walk-in traffic isn't quite back to where it was, but it's certainly better than it was when they were at our front door. They're not as aggressive with our patients—they don't scream at them any more—but they're just as determined as ever. The front desk tells me that about half of our patients still complain about feeling threatened."

"But it's better than it was?"

"Better, yes. Ideal, no. A week ago, somebody splattered red paint on our door and the windows out front. We've got a couple of parking spaces in the alley out back. One of our volunteers had a flat tire and the guy who fixed it said somebody had slashed it. Somebody heaved a rock through the back window of my car. We can't prove anything, but there's not much doubt about who's behind that stuff. We've put a security service on retainer, they patrol the alley now and then and that helps, but we're all feeling vulnerable even with that."

Emily paused to jot some notes.

"I'm still collecting background," she said, "but I'm planning to come back with my camera guy once I have a better sense of the story. Will you be okay talking about the vandalism when we do that?"

"Of course."

"When I interviewed Ms. Howorth, I asked if some clients might be willing to talk with me. She said she'd see if that could be arranged. Would you object to that?"

"Not if they agree," said Joan with a quick smile. "After all, we're in the business of giving women choices."

"Yes, you are. Now, if this is too personal, say so, but do the harshest comments—you know, 'murderer,' 'baby killer,'—get to you?"

"I can't say I enjoy hearing those words, but ultimately, it isn't my choice to terminate a pregnancy and when that choice is made, I don't believe 'murder' is accurate. Or fair. The patient makes the choice and I don't have a moment's doubt about her right to do exactly that. I know how the anti-crowd feels—we get a few nasty, ugly letters most days—and I try to respect their point of view, but I can't tolerate a society in which women are treated as slaves."

"That's a strong word."

"It's accurate. If RTLC gets their way, women will be subjugated. They want to impose second class status on us. There's not much which is more offensive, at least to me, than the notion that men can exercise total control over women's bodies."

"Some of RTLC's leadership are women."

"But most of those in power aren't," said Estrada. "We're not even close to having decent representation in legislatures, never mind fifty-two percent. If men got pregnant, abortion would be as common as buying a box of tissues when you have a cold. For me, it's about equality, pure and simple. Women aren't inferior, despite what a lot of men think."

Emily paused once more to write notes.

"I don't mean to sound harsh," said Joan. "It's not my style, but I've given up being placid about this issue. The other side isn't going to back down, so our only option is to stand as firmly as they do."

She glanced at her watch.

"I'm sorry, but the clinic opens soon. I need to get the examination rooms ready and I have patient files to review before they walk in the door. I'm happy to make more time for you, but right now I have to go to work."

"I understand. When I'm ready to put the piece together, I'll get back to you. Maybe you and Carmen could do a joint interview—that would save you both some time."

"If you can find a way to do that, I'm ready. Fact is, Carmen and I make appointments with each other just so we can keep up with everything. Ridiculous, isn't it? Her desk is right there"—she pointed one desk over—"and if we get ten minutes a day to talk, it's a miracle."

"It was just a thought," said Emily. "Thanks so much for your time."

"Anytime," said Joan. "Well, any time when I can find the time, at least."

She rose from her chair and walked around the desk. The two women faced one another at eye level.

"I have one more question," said Emily.

"Shoot."

"Don't be offended, but do they really call you Dr. J?"

Estrada grinned.

"I'm a lot shorter than the other one, for sure. But you oughta see my outside jump shot."

"I'm sure it's great," said Emily. "At least they don't call you 'Shorty.'"

"You get that, too?"

"Often," said Emily, laughing, "But I have a steadfast rule. One and done—I only give them one shot at it."

"Hmm, good idea. I usually just suffer it."

Estrada sat and opened the first of a stack of files on her desk. Emily stowed her notepad and shouldered her satchel. She turned to leave and then turned back again.

"I have a thought," she said.

Joan looked up.

"There's a bunch of us, women in professions, mostly media, we meet at Riccardo's on Friday evenings. I think you'd like the group. Ms. Howorth, too. If you guys would like to join us, it might be fun."

"Fridays," said Estrada. "Riccardo's. I can't make a promise, but it does sound interesting. Thanks."

"My pleasure," said Emily.

"Bert, we have a problem."

Bert Presley was at his desk, jotting notes on what appeared to Emily, looking at it upside down, to be a set of balance sheets.

"I'll say," said Bert. "We're spending too much. Malafronte thinks we may have to make some cuts. I can't find anything to cut which won't put a serious hitch in our giddy-up."

"I'm just a lowly reporter," said Emily, "high finance is beyond my reach."

"So are books on the top shelf."

"Cute, Bert. You get one short joke a month. That was it."

"Sorry, couldn't resist. What's up? What problem?"

"First, I'm here because I didn't want to bring this up in the morning planning meeting."

"Okay," said Bert with a mild grimace, "this sounds like something I'm not gonna like."

"Probably not. I've been working on the surveillance camera story."

"Good."

"Some good. I talked to a contact at U. Chicago's law school. He says there's not a privacy issue with these things because there is no expectation of privacy in public spaces. In the house, a doctor's office, talking to legal counsel, yes, but pumping gas or shopping at the mall, no."

"And that's a problem?"

"I'm not there yet. I went out to Schaumburg to watch a couple of guys install a camera system. They wouldn't talk to me. I had a chat with the guy, runs the shop, and he wasn't keen on doing an interview. I can probably talk him into it and, maybe, get a couple of customers to chime in, but I don't think we're going to get that far."

"Why not?"

"Here's the problem, Bert. The station owner gave me the brochure the company left for him to read. They're called Bad Guy Eyes—"

"You're kidding."

"Could I make that up? That's the name. I made a couple of calls, sniffed around to find out who runs the place. Talked to the receptionist over there, too. My thought was, we'd get the owner or whoever's in charge to sit for an interview."

"That makes sense."

"It did until I found out who owns the operation."

"Yeah?"

"Bert, I'm sorry, but I don't see how we can do a story about Bad Guy Eyes."

Presley frowned. "Why?"

"Because the president of the company is Don's son-in-law."

"Don Malafronte?"

"Yes."

Presley's face went crimson and his eyes betrayed a level of anger which made Emily nervous.

"That sonuva—are you telling me Don wanted us to do a story about his own family's business?"

"It's even worse. The receptionist at Bad Guy Eye—they call her Margie—is Margaret Cunningham. She was Margaret Malafronte until she got married."

Presley picked up the spread sheets and tamped them until they were perfectly aligned. He set them aside, folded his hands, drew several deep breaths, his eyes closed, and then slowly shook his head from side to side.

"You're right. We have to spike the story."

"What about—"

"I'll deal with Don. Right away. Go back to your desk."

"Okay."

Emily turned to leave.

"Sorry, Bert."

"You had no choice, Emily. I'd be furious if you hadn't told me. You did the right thing."

"I know that," she said, "but I'm still sorry."

"Yeah."

She was at the door.

"One more thing, Winter."

"Yes?"

"I understand why you didn't want to raise this in the meeting, in front of everybody. It would have put Don in a terrible position—embarrass him, shame him. You protected him and you get high marks for that. Thanks."

———————

"Gracious, that's a major breach of ethics," said Ben. "Quite astonishing. Do you think they'll fire him?"

"I don't know. For a moment there, Bert was as angry as I've ever seen him. He said he was going to talk to Don right away, but that's the last I heard."

"Did Malafronte think you wouldn't find out? That you'd miss the connection, or maybe ignore it?"

"I'm not sure he thought about it at all. He's a decent guy. I guess he thought it wasn't important or maybe he was just trying to help his son-in-law's business grow. You know, being a doting dad, making sure his daughter would be well cared for. And, after all, he's not a journalist, he's a business-side suit. He may not have seen anything amiss because he just didn't know better."

"You are often too generous, m'love. The man wanted to compromise the ethics of a reputable newsroom. The newsroom he manages. Tis hardly an innocent initiative."

"Bert killed the story as soon as I told him, so we weren't compromised at all."

"Thanks to you and Presley."

They were at their dining room table. The temperature had risen to the high eighties with humidity well over fifty percent, muggy enough to justify the quiet hum of the air conditioner in the living room window. Ben had cooked a rack of ribs while Emily created a salad and scooped coleslaw into a serving dish. There was a Shearing record on the turntable. Emily was pleased to be at home, something of a Saturday night rarity.

"I was discouraged when I learned what Malafronte had done," said Emily. "I seem to keep banging up against integrity issues these days."

"More than one?"

"I interviewed Joan Estrada yesterday and ran into the same quandary I had with Carmen Howorth."

"I recall," said Ben. "You feared a breach of ethics, yes? Concerns regarding stepping over the line."

"I stomped on it with Dr. J."

"How?"

"Well, first, I really liked her. In other circumstances, she'd be a pal. She's smart and sassy and dedicated to her work—"

"Traits I know and love," said Ben.

"Hush. The thing is, Ben, I believe she and Carmen and the others at the clinic are absolutely right. If I didn't have the job I do, I'd be contributing to their work in every way possible."

"There's nothing wrong with advancing women's rights," said Ben. "You do that all the time just by doing what you do. Most of your cohorts on the Rules Committee do, too—when you do your jobs, you're all creating a new paradigm, workplaces in which women are as equal and as capable as men."

"Yes, I see that. But an important part of my

job is remaining objective, reporting without bias. I'm having trouble balancing objectivity with my own beliefs."

Ben gazed out the window for a moment.

"I don't think perfection is attainable. For instance, when Gary Easton was covering crime for your station, his support for the cops on the beat was overt; the man never heard an allegation he didn't believe. When Lois Lipton covered the RTLC hearing, she didn't leave her feminist principles at the door, right? She just didn't let them get in the way.

"The key is to recognize the bias and make every effort to curb it. The more passionate your feeling, the harder you have to work at it. It seems to me that you're doing exactly that. You've identified your bias—twice now—which means that you're aware of it. Bad reporters just ignore the conflict—assuming they even see one—whereas you identify and confront it. I don't think the practice of journalism requires more than that."

"I'm still uncomfortable," said Emily. "I invited Estrada and Howorth to drop in on the Rules Committee—they could end up being friends, part of my circle."

"And I do not doubt that, should that occur, it will only strengthen your resolve to be vigilant about your biases. So long as your reporting is balanced, if you recognize your prejudices and compensate for them, there can be no harm."

"You make it sound easy."

"To the contrary, m'love. I imagine it's the hardest part of your work. When all is said and done, you're required to maintain objectivity even as your instincts run counter to that requirement. You recall that I had the same quandary representing RTLC—the effort to set one's most cherished principles aside in order to be fair is supremely difficult."

"You are a treasure, sir. I don't know how you do it, but you always find a way to make me, what? Better? Stronger? Wiser, maybe."

"Poppycock! All I do is listen and respond. You're the one who raised the concerns, after all. I just pay attention and offer the occasional observation."

"In this case, the observation is extremely astute, Ben. Thanks. And, for the record, may I just note that I have taken what you said to heart even as I am entirely distracted by the fact that you have a sizable dollop of barbecue sauce on your lower lip."

"Heaven forfend! Shall I wipe it away, or would you prefer to come over here and make it vanish?"

"I'd have to kiss you to do that," said Emily.

"Ah, well, that begs the question."

"Which is?"

"What are you waiting for?"

Chapter Seven

The phone rang at six thirty-five on Monday morning. Ben was already in the shower, scheduled to be at a litigation strategy session by eight o'clock. Emily hesitated, reluctant to give up the luxury of sprawling across the bed and burying her face in Ben's pillow, his scent still lingering on it. She picked up the phone after four rings.

"Emily, it's Bert. I need you to get over to Clark Street as fast as you can."

"Bert? It's so early. What's going on?"

"Somebody firebombed the Northside Women's Care Clinic. Fire department, cops are on the scene. City News wire says it's a lot of damage. You're closest to it, get over there now. I'm calling Kern soon as I hang up, he'll meet you there."

Emily rapidly dressed, combed her hair and grabbed her satchel. She had her hand on the front doorknob before she realized Ben would come out of the shower and find her missing. She trotted back to the master bath and told him about the call, then raced back down the hall before he could ask any questions.

She quickly walked down Wellington to Sheridan and turned right, headed for Belmont. There was a hotel on the corner which sometimes had a cab or two waiting. The cab driver she snagged was not happy with her destination; he'd been hoping for a run to O'Hare, not a quick trip down the street and a few clocks north. As it turned out, he was even crankier when they approached the NWCC building and found the area blocked—his short ride became even shorter and he grumbled about that, too. Thinking of Uncle Max, Emily tipped him anyhow.

She clipped her ID badge to her blazer and dashed down the street, slowing as she passed the first of the fire trucks. She surveyed the scene as she edged forward, dodging firemen and hoses. The fire was almost out, but the storefront was still smoldering and smoke was hanging in the air. The smell was foreboding. Dozens of uniformed men moved rapidly in several directions. Emily admired their coordinated cooperation—every man was in a hurry but none impeded any other's progress.

Bert's information was accurate; the damage was substantial. Both large windows at the front of the storefront were blown out, parts of the roof had fallen and other sections looked precariously close to collapsing. The wall supporting the window on the right had caved and some of the plastic chairs in the waiting area had become eerily warped in the heat. The reception area was blackened and the wall behind the desk was scorched. The few posters still hanging from walls were soaked and laden with ash. The desk was filthy from soot, smoke and water.

The damage on the left side was more severe. Most of the ceiling had collapsed onto exam tables in the patient cubicles, the white walls and the sheets on the exam tables were black. There was an enormous jagged hole in a wall near the center of the clinic space. There was no surface from which water was not dripping; everything bore grim evidence of raging flames and horrendous heat. As she surveyed it all, Emily's first thought was that nobody would be coming to this facility for a long, long time.

She turned and scanned a sizable group of men standing in the street in front of the clinic. They were far enough removed to be out of the way of those attending the remnants of the fire but close enough to watch as they talked. Emily recognized two of the men and headed for the group.

Gary Easton saw her coming and turned his back to her. Jack Potter said something to the man on his right and stepped forward to greet her.

"Hey, Nails. You're slipping. That guy over there, in khakis, navy blazer, he's from the *Trib*. You're not first on the scene."

"Cab couldn't get close enough, Jack. I had to walk a couple of blocks. Why are you here?"

"Good to see you, too. I'm on the job."

Emily's face fell.

"You're still working homicide, right?"

"Yup."

"Then—"

"One casualty, Emily. A woman was working in the left side of the building. Not quite sure what happened, but she's dead."

"Do you have an ID?"

Potter turned and took a plastic envelope from one of the men standing behind him. He examined it and then held it up to show Emily.

"Joan Estrada. MD. She was the clinic's—"

"Medical director," said Emily.

A powerful force swept through her and she staggered back. Potter reached out and took an arm, steadying her. When she straightened herself, she glanced again at the ID badge in the bag and turned to look up to Potter. There were tears in her eyes.

"You knew her? I'm so sorry, I had no idea."

Emily nodded. She started to say something but the words caught in her throat. She coughed and nodded again.

"You want to sit for a moment, kiddo? There's a bus kiosk, we're using it as sort of a command post but you're welcome—"

Emily took a deep breath. "Thank you, no, Jack. I've got work to do."

She dug into her satchel and pulled out a notepad and a pen.

"Tell me what you know."

"Two Molotov cocktails, one through each front window. The arson guy from CFD says he thinks they were large jugs, maybe bottles, high octane gas, rags stuffed in the top of each bottle as the trigger. It's not clear why, but the damage on the left side of the building—"

"The clinic side," said Emily.

"That's what the debris looks like, yes. That side got the worst of it. The arson guy thinks something else fed the fire on that side. He's still in there trying to figure it out."

"Witnesses?"

"None we've found. The cocktails were probably thrown at about six o'clock in the morning, maybe a few minutes earlier. The fire department got the first call just after six, several more came right after the first one. Most of the callers reported an explosion, not a fire. None of these shops"—Potter swept his arm up and down the block—"were open, nobody inside when we canvased. There must have been some traffic, of course, but anybody with half a brain would floor the gas and speed away. If there were people walking near here, they probably took off too, as soon as they heard something or saw the flames. At that hour, you wouldn't expect a lot of pedestrians in any case."

"You'll be here a while? My camera guy's on his way."

Potter grimaced.

"I'll be here, but it won't do you any good."

"Why not?"

Potter pointed back to the group of men.

"Gary Easton's here. He's coordinating with the FD station chief, but if anybody wants interviews,

Gary's made it real clear that he'll be handling the press. When more of you show up, he says he'll do a briefing for everyone."

Emily looked over Potter's shoulder and spotted Easton. She caught his eye and he smirked, shook his head once and turned his attention to the others in his group.

"Gary doesn't look like he's happy to see me."

"Now, there's a surprise," said Potter.

Gary Easton had been WSMP's crime reporter when Emily started working for the station. When she had pushed Bert Presley and Donald Malafronte to cover a murder in addition to the soft feature stories she'd been hired to deliver, Easton had bridled and sabotaged her efforts at every turn. Eventually, Emily scooped him on the murder story, filming the murderer's confession and arrest; Jack Potter had been the arresting officer. Her work thoroughly debunked Easton's version of the murder which had been fed to him by the police department; it was deliberately misleading and Emily's work exposed it as entirely false. Easton responded badly and quit his job, moving from a reporter covering the police to a post as the police department's in-house media relations representative.

Scott Kern arrived and Emily walked back to the clinic site with him. At her direction, he filmed the destruction from the sidewalk.

"I want something better," Kern said. "You stay put."

He ducked under the yellow tape perimeter and carefully picked his way through the debris and around the hoses and firemen, shooting as he did so. He was agile enough to stay out of the way as he shot for two or three minutes and then returned.

"Nasty in there," he said. "Good thing it wasn't occupied."

"It was," said Emily and tears filled her eyes once more. "The clinic's doctor was killed."

"Wow. So, it's arson and murder?"

"Yes," said Emily, her jaw tight. "Murder."

There was a pay phone on the sidewalk across the street, in front of a large drug store, and Emily used it to call Bert Presley.

"I've got the basics," she said, "I can do a stand-up and then voice-over the film Scott's got—he went inside and got some good visuals."

"Interviews?"

"The fire department's arson guy is still searching the scene. Once he's done, I'll try to corner him. There are a couple of homicide guys here—"

"Wait. Homicide?"

"The clinic's medical director was in the building. She's dead."

"Lord."

"One of them is Jack Potter, he's great on camera, but I can't use him. CPD has a spokesperson on site."

Emily let it hang and Bert took a beat before he spoke.

"Easton?"

"Easton."

"Sorry," said Bert. "You'll just have to suck it up,

Emily. I'll take your stand-up and Scott's b-roll now, as soon as you shoot the stand-up. I'll have one of the interns run over to pick it up. We'll put it up as soon as we edit. You and Scott stay, get some interviews, keep digging for new angles. Call me if you get anything else we can use—we're probably going to extend the morning newscast, so if you can get something quick, we'll use it in that extra hour. If not, it'll still be fresh for the Nooner. Any questions?"

"No."

"Good. Go to work."

The intern arrived as Emily was wrapping up her report. Kern turned over his b-roll tape of the destruction and Emily's stand-up and told the intern to get it back to the studio "ten minutes ago." He spotted a diner down the street which appeared to be open and left to get coffee and a muffin for each of them.

Emily used the break to wander down the sidewalk until she was well removed from the police and firemen. She leaned against the wall of a dry-cleaning shop, closed her eyes and let the horror take her. The violent damage to the building and the death of a woman she admired felt like racing rust, corroding her from the inside out. The stench of the smoke and the havoc it represented was inescapable and enervating.

She focused on the cause of the destruction and the death, seeking any explanation other than the one which she viewed as a certainty. Firebombing the clinic was deliberate and calculated; it could only be the work of those who viewed the clinic and its mission as intolerable. Her shock at the destruction she had witnessed gave way, inexorably, to a torrent of anger. When Scott approached with her coffee, he saw her face and stopped in his tracks, backing away and then turning his back to her.

A few minutes later, Emily leveraged herself away from the wall and walked over to stand with Kern.

"You okay?"

"I've had far better days, Scott," she said.

"You were glaring at me, you know. I've never seen you angry. It's scary."

"Oh, no, Scott. I mean, I didn't intend to—I wasn't really looking at you. It's just that this—I am angry, but not with you. Sorry, really."

"It's okay. So, let's see if we can find a place to sit for a second, have some joe, grab a bite."

"No," said Emily. She tore a hunk of muffin away and wolfed it down, following it with two quick gulps of coffee. "I want to get back to this. Right now."

"You sure? You're upset. Taking a little break won't hurt—it'll all be here when you're ready. The fire crew has a lot to do, they aren't going anywhere anytime soon."

"Now, Scott. We have a lot of work to do."

"Okay."

"Eat your muffin—"

"It's a doughnut."

"Eat it and let's get to it. We have a murder to solve."

Chapter Eight

"Our department is scouring the surrounding area for evidence and witnesses. The fire department's arson investigation team is continuing to search the building for evidence. We can confirm that at least two fire bombs were thrown into the structure and that the structural damage makes the building uninhabitable. There was one fatality, Dr. Joan Estrada, the medical director of the Northside Women's Care Clinic. The exact cause of death will not be disclosed until we have conducted our investigation and an autopsy has been performed, but there is no doubt that she was a victim of the bombing."

Gary Easton stood before half a dozen microphones and camera crews. Two still photographers were shooting and there were at least six print reporters on the scene as well. Emily was standing in the group of reporters. When she raised her hand, Easton looked directly at her and said, "Jerry."

The *Sun-Times* reporter leaned in.

"Gary, do you have any information about potential suspects?"

"Not at this time."

Emily raised her hand again.

"Bob," said Easton. "You're up."

"You said 'at least two' firebombs. Do you believe there were more?"

"The investigation is ongoing, but the damage to one side of the building suggests that something more than a firebomb was involved."

"When you say firebomb, are you referring to Molotov cocktails?"

"The arson team believes two glass containers filled with gasoline were thrown into the building. There is evidence that rags soaked in gas were stuffed into the bottle necks. The perp lit the rags and threw the bottles in. When the glass containers broke, the fire spread instantly. We estimate the containers were large enough to contain at least a gallon of gas, maybe more. The containers went through the front windows. So, yes, the preliminary evidence suggests at least two Molotov cocktails."

Emily raised her hand. "Gary?"

Easton ignored her.

"That's all we have for now. The investigation continues and when we have more for you, we'll either come back here for an update or release new information through the CPD press office. Thank you."

Several reporters shouted questions, but Easton turned away. He walked around the battery of microphones and through the reporters. When he passed Emily, he slowed just a little and spoke in a voice just above a whisper.

"Good luck covering this one, Winter."

Emily and Kern shot a recap of her earlier report with the destroyed building just behind her as she spoke. Scott Kern panned away to the rubble and smoke, returning to her as she wrapped up. She called Bert and arranged for another round of pick-up and delivery.

"There are two cuts from Easton I think will work, Bert. Easton's first three sentences are a solid summary of the crime and investigation, use that. Later, he describes how the firebombs worked, in the bite where he uses 'Molotov cocktail.' That's descriptive. You might use it behind the b-roll we sent over earlier—Easton describing the cocktails while we show the damage they did."

"Got it," said Presley. "Here's the deal. Before you hang up, put Kern on the line. I'm sending him to cover a couple of other stories for the evening 'cast, but I want you to stay. Keep digging. I'm going to send the broadcast truck over there. At noon and for all the evening 'casts, 5:00 p.m., 6:00 p.m. and 6:30 p.m., you'll go live. Make the 6:30 p.m. hit as tight as you can. Unless something breaks after that, we'll use it again at ten. Got it?"

"Yes."

"Anything else?"

Emily thought for a moment.

"In the top right-hand drawer of my desk, there's a red plastic bag, it's got a zipper on it. Send it over in the remote truck, ask them to give it to me."

"Red plastic bag. What's—oh, wait, I know. Makeup."

"Yes. And, one more thing. There's a dark blue garment bag, it's got my name on an ID tag, hanging in the corner of my cubicle. There's a plain oxford blue blouse in it and an extra Team 8 blazer. Send them over, too."

"Blue blouse, blazer, red plastic bag. That it?"

"That's it. I've got soot all over everything I'm wearing and Scott noticed a smudge of smoke on my chin. He didn't tell me about it until we'd shot everything—he thinks it showed that we're live on the scene. I don't have a mirror handy, but I'm looking at my reflection in this store window and I look pretty horrible. I'd like to clean up for the evening 'casts."

"Done. It's too bad we can't televise odor, isn't it?"

"What are you talking about?"

"I've covered my share of fires and it doesn't take long before you start to smell like a fireplace. I bet you do. If we had smell-o-vision, they'd know you're on the scene for sure."

"Boy, you sure know how to flatter a girl, don't you?"

"You're on a tough, demanding assignment, Winter. I'm just trying to lighten the load a little."

"'Preciate it, Bert. I'll call in before you go live at noon."

By 9:30 a.m., there were several large vehicles in the drugstore parking lot across the street from the clinic, each with an ungainly antenna rising above the roof. They all had cables strung from truck to cameras placed so reporters could file stories with the burnt-out clinic in the background. At noon, when a few of the stations broadcast half-hour newscasts, smoke was still drifting from and around what remained of the building. Print reporters and photographers worked the area as well; two of the reporters had two-way radio equipment in their cars so they could report back to their editors or copy desks; the rest of the print people took turns using the lone pay phone at the drugstore.

Emily interviewed a couple of shop owners on the block and then walked around the corner and into an apartment building. She went in and walked up the stairs until she was on the fourth floor. She calculated which of the units on that floor had windows facing Clark Street and began knocking on doors. Most were empty, but she talked to an elderly woman who had been awakened by the noise and a middle-aged man who was getting ready to walk his dog when he heard what he called "a big bang." He had gone to the window and seen the billowing flames; he was one of those who had called the fire in shortly after it erupted. Kern had left and the remote truck hadn't arrived, so she took copious notes and secured names and phone numbers.

She went back to the street and found Jack Potter.

"Jack, have you heard anything from the arson team?"

"Not yet," he said. "Their primary guy—cat named Sean Sheehan—is still in there. I'll give him this, he's as thorough as I am when I'm at a scene. He's not going to miss anything."

Emily looked across the street.

"Which one is he?"

"He's in the front area on the right—got a fireman's protective slicker on, but no helmet. See the guy, bending over that melted chair, red hair?"

"I think so. On the far right, just inside where the window was?"

"That's the guy."

"Thanks. I'll keep an eye on him."

"'Kay. Sorry I can't help you with stuff for airing, but Easton went out of his way to warn me not to give you an interview."

"Me personally?"

Potter grinned.

"He said 'You give your pal Winter one second of sound, I'll make sure you get to spend the rest of your career in the overnight press room.'"

"He knows how to hit below the belt, doesn't he? You hated that job."

"Not as much as you did, but yeah, it's a threat I respect enough to play ball with him."

"Makes you feel any better, you can take my word for it—the man's an idiot."

"Roger that."

"So, Easton didn't say we can't talk to each other, did he?"

"Nope."

"Good. Can I assume you'll be looking hard at RTLC?"

"That the group's been picketing this place for, what, a month or more?"

"Yes."

"Then yeah, they'll be high on the list. You got any leads I should know about?"

"I've talked with three of them. Carol Lobes and Norman Brent, they pretty much run the operation. And a kid, just out of high school, named Sam Terhune. He's not exactly a fan of the clinic and it's personal with him. I'm not sure he's up to something like this, but you might want to have a chat with him. He was angry the way teens can be."

Potter took notes.

"Anyone else?"

"Not yet, but I'm going to work this story as hard and as fast as I can, so there may be more."

"You'll share?"

"Of course."

"Good. Thanks."

"One more question, Jack."

"Shoot."

"Easton still here?"

Potter smiled.

"Nah. He did his dog and pony show for the cameras and spent a little more time with the print folks. Did a couple of one-on-one's with the radio news guys and then he took off."

"Good to know," said Emily. "When the cat's away—"

"Got it. If you can make him unhappy, it'll make me smile."

"Oh, I think you can count on that, Jack."

Emily left him and walked over to one of the fire trucks where she chatted with two of the rank and file. She got them to give her useful quotes—"One of the meanest I've ever seen" and "This place went up in a hurry." She got their names and thanked them. While she worked, she glanced back at the clinic often, making sure that the arson investigator was still working in the ravaged building.

A few minutes after the WSMP truck pulled into the parking lot, Emily saw Sean Sheehan come onto the sidewalk and shed his heavy protective gear. She dashed across the street and approached him.

"Mr. Sheehan, I'm Emily Winter, WSMP News. Can you give me a quick report on what your investigation told you?"

"Sure, but not until I find a bottle of water."

Emily dug into her satchel and pulled out a plastic bottle.

"Here."

"Geez, that's impressive. Any chance you got a shot of brandy or a couple of beers in there, too?"

Emily laughed.

"Not even coffee."

He uncapped the bottle and drained it in a single long pull, belched once and leaned back against a fender on the nearest fire truck.

"That's better. Thanks. You never get used to the air after one of these."

"So, what did you find?"

"An exploded oxygen tank."

"I don't understand."

"I'll give you a crash course. A good Molotov Cocktail will generate something close to 500 degrees of heat right after the bottle explodes and the gas ignites. Oxygen burns at about 125 degrees. In this case, the second cocktail—the first one went into the front window on the right, the second one on the left—landed just a few feet from an oxygen tank, the kind they use in hospitals. The tank got soaked with gas and when the flames took hold, it exploded, probably in less than a minute. It sent shrapnel all over the place. The lady in there was not far from the tank. I don't think she would have survived in any event, but when that tank blew, it threw three or four good sized shards at her. One of them caught her dead center, in the chest. Coroner will confirm it, but I think she probably died instantly."

Emily drew a long ragged breath and she fought down an impulse to scream. She took a moment to compose herself.

"So there's no doubt that Dr. Estrada was murdered."

"Not as far as I'm concerned. Whoever did this might as well have put two or three rounds into her. I apologize for being crude, but I'm convinced she was dead before she hit the floor."

"My crew just arrived. Could I ask you to walk over there with me and do an interview?"

"I can't do that," he said. "I'm headed back to file my report, the brass will see it and then they'll decide how to put it out. They'll probably let CPD handle it—it's a homicide, so it's a cop case; I'm just the expert they'll use when they take the bastard who did this to trial."

"I understand. I won't compromise you, but I'm going to use what you've told me. It's an important part of the story."

"I'm not in your business, ma'am, but I'd say it *is* the story. Still, I have to play by the rules."

"Of course you do."

"There's one other thing," said Sheehan. "That guy, the one in that ridiculous gangster movie hat, who does press for the cops—"

"Gary Easton."

"He's the one. He told us nobody gives anything to reporters he hasn't cleared first. I thought he was something of a prig, but, like I say, I try to play by the rules."

"I try, too," said Emily, "but sometimes, I don't try very hard."

"Good for you," he said. "But if you use my name, I'll be damn near as angry with you as I am with whoever did this."

"I'm sorry," said Emily, with a tiny twinkle in her eye, "but I'm not sure I got your name."

Killer Cocktail

Joel Bellman

Good Evening, Chicago. I'm Joel Bellman, WSMP Team 8 News.

Brent Hopkins

And I'm Brent Hopkins. Tonight's lead story—the Northside Women's Care Clinic was destroyed in an early morning fire which both the Chicago police and fire departments have confirmed was the result of firebombs thrown into the front windows of the clinic's facility on Clark Street. Our Emily Winter is on the scene with the latest details. Emily. . .

Winter

Brent, Team 8 News has learned exclusively that the death of Doctor Joan Estrada, NWCC's medical director, occurred when one of two Molotov cocktails thrown into the building caused an oxygen tank to explode. Dr. Estrada died instantly when shrapnel from the oxygen tank struck her in the chest. Our sources believe that she died instantly.

We have also learned that the two Molotov cocktails contained large amounts of high octane gasoline. One of the firefighters at the scene said it is the meanest fire he's ever seen. Witnesses in nearby apartment buildings tell us that the explosion was loud enough to be heard at least a block away. Flames and smoke from the fire could be seen from at least a mile away and, as you can see behind me, the building is still smoldering. One fire crew remains in place to make sure the fire is completely knocked down.

The police department has yet to identify any suspects in this horrific attack, but the clinic has been the object of several weeks of demonstrations by an organization which is opposed to NWCC's advocacy of abortion as a woman's choice.

For more, we'll go back to Joel Bellman. He has a statement from Chicago police spokesman Gary Easton. For Team 8 News, I'm Emily Solomon Winter. Joel. . .

Chapter Nine

"Just so you know," said Bert Presley, "Don Malafronte won't be coming to our meetings for an extended period. Don's working on budget issues and management has asked him to review our overall public affairs efforts, so his plate is kinda full."

Presley paused for a moment, waiting for any response, and when none came he gave Emily a quick nod—she thought he was signaling approval—and resumed.

"First up, of course, is the NWCC bombing, but before we get to assignments, I want to give Winter her due. She delivered an exclusive, the fact that it was an exploding oxygen tank which killed the victim. Nobody else had that story yesterday, but it's front page in the *Trib* this morning. Nice job, Emily."

There was a smattering of applause and a "way to go" from a producer; Presley gave her a little salute.

"Okay, let's move along. We need to follow up with the cops and Sean Sheehan, the arson investigator, to see if they've uncovered anything new. The wire budget says there's going to be a joint press conference at City Hall, the Mayor, several Aldermen, probably the city attorney, mid-morning. We need reaction from NWCC—maybe the Executive Director or somebody from their board. Have they considered what's next, will they stay open, that sort of thing."

Emily raised her hand.

"We should talk to RTLC, too, Bert. Even if there's no connection to the bombing, they've been hectoring the clinic steadily for weeks—it would be good to get a response from them."

"That was next on my list. So, we'll need at least a couple of you working it today. Stone, you reach out to the cops and fire department first thing, then head over to the Hall to cover that. If the cops or fire people have something new, you can get them after you cover the Hall.

"Winter, you take NWCC—"

"I've got a contact on their board and I can probably get to Carmen Howorth. I can reach out to the RTLC contacts I have, too."

"That's good."

One of the noon news producers raised her hand. "Bert, can I make a suggestion?"

"Shoot."

"Gary Easton's the only one at the cop shop we can use, right? We all know he's not exactly our biggest fan for starters, but if you use Stone, it'll be even less productive—he doesn't think women belong in news. And he wouldn't even acknowledge

Emily yesterday at the briefing."

"Well, you have to admit, that's gotta be personal," said Presley.

"I know he's got a thing for Emily, but the point remains. It might be better if we send one of the guys—maybe have Bellman or Hopkins reach out?"

Presley nodded and scowled.

"I get that. But I'm not about to let Easton—or anybody else, for that matter—dictate how we do our jobs. That's part of the reason Malafronte—no, forget that. If Easton shuts us out, we'll take whatever City News gets from him and give it to the anchor desk, but I'm sending Stone. I decide how we cover the news. I want Easton to know who controls this newsroom. He sure as hell doesn't."

There was a moment's silence as the room absorbed the gravity with which Presley spoke.

"Damn right, boss," said one of the producers. "Most of us never liked that guy anyhow."

"Bert," said Emily, "I'm shocked."

"Nobody tells us how to cover—"

"No, it's not that," said Emily. "You're absolutely right about that. It's just that, unless I'm hearing things, you just sounded a whole lot like a real feminist."

"I've been called worse," said Presley. "Now I think about it, coming from you, it's a compliment."

Emily turned to Nikki Stone. "Do not use my name if you can get to Easton, but it may help with Sean Sheehan. Get all you can from Sheehan in the news conference—after that, Easton will probably shut him down so he's the star."

"Got it," said Nikki.

Presley worked through the balance of the day's assignments and the meeting broke up. Emily went to her desk, opened her notepad and began making calls.

"Carmen, it's Emily Winter."

"Hello. I remember you."

Her voice was ragged and there was no energy in her greeting.

"I know you must be devastated and I'm sorry to intrude, but we'd like an interview if you're up to it. Perhaps later this morning?"

"I can't," said Howorth. "I'm sorry, but—"

"I understand. I won't keep you long. We'd like to ask you about yesterday's. . .about the attack."

"I don't have time for you because our board is meeting, by phone, in a few minutes. We have so much to do. We must plan a memorial service and figure out what to do for our patients. It's all so overwhelming."

"Would it be easier if I talk with Alicia Good? I know she's on the board. She and I are pals."

"I'll suggest that to the board. I'm sure it'll be okay."

"Thanks. Let's do this—when the meeting is over, ask her to give me a call. I'll be at my desk or she can leave a message and I'll connect with her when I'm free."

"That's fine. I'm normally the spokesperson, but in this case, I just, I'm not ready. I'm feeling lost. Alone. Empty."

"I can only imagine," said Emily. "I'll let you go.

Have Alicia call me when she's ready. Goodbye."

"Goodbye."

Carol Lobes did not answer her phone.

The message on Norman Brent's phone said he wasn't available, but he promised to return all calls. Emily left her number and requested an interview.

She flipped through her notes and came across Carol Lobes' reference to Jon Haskill, the man with the deep pockets who donated a lot to RTLC. She lifted a directory from one of her desk drawers and found two listings, one for a residence in Skokie and, in the yellow pages, a basic listing for his company.

"Good morning, this is Emily Winter, with WSMP News. I'm hoping that Mr. Haskill can make himself available for an interview about yesterday's bombing at the Northside Women's Care Clinic."

"Whatever for? He has nothing to do with—"

"It's our understanding that he is a supporter, a generous donor, of Right To Life Chicago. Since RTLC has been picketing the clinic for several weeks, we'd like to talk with someone associated with them about their reaction to the bombing."

"I don't know anything about that," she said.

"Is he in?"

"Yes, he's here, but I'm pretty sure he won't—"

"Could you please tell him I'm on the line?"

"I don't think...no. I'm sure he won't take your call."

"No offense. I'm sure you're just doing your job, but could you just let him know I'm on the line, waiting?"

There was a pause. Emily could almost see the

woman struggling with her choices.

"It's important," said Emily. "Everyone knows about the demonstrations and the court case, people will probably draw conclusions. They may even see a connection. Silence won't do Mr. Haskill's group any favors. Shouldn't the public know that they weren't involved? Or that they are as shocked by the attack as the rest of the city is?"

There was a long pause.

"Please hold."

Emily cradled the phone on her shoulder and spread the *Tribune* across her desk. She read the paper's coverage of the bombing; it was extensive and featured several dramatic photos of the destruction and a photo of Joan Estrada taken at a fundraising event. She moved to other stories and was finishing the front section when the receptionist came back on the line.

"Mr. Haskill is not available," she said, "but he understands your concern. He suggests that you contact either Carol Lobes or Norman Brent—"

"I've done that. I—"

"He authorized me to provide you with phone numbers for both of them."

"I have those numbers," said Emily. "I haven't been able to reach them and I don't want our coverage to be one-sided. Perhaps we could arrange for something tomorrow."

The receptionist let out a grim chuckle.

"I don't think so," she said. "He really doesn't want to be involved. At all."

"I understand," said Emily. "But I hope you'll let him know that I may be in touch again, probably sooner rather than later. We aren't going to let this story go and RTLC is part of it."

"That may be so," she said, "but when I spoke to him, just now, he was very clear that he has nothing to say to you. It's not personal—he said he won't talk to anybody about this."

"At least for now," said Emily. "Please tell him I'll be in touch again."

"Good luck," the receptionist said. "I'm telling you, there's no chance."

"We'll see."

Emily sat and gazed at the ceiling, frustrated, discouraged and determined to move forward despite the roadblocks she'd encountered with each successive phone call. She impatiently flipped the pages of her notepad back and forth, scanning for any other possible leads. She saw Sam Terhune's name, said "Aha!" to herself and dialed yet another number.

"Hello."

"Hi. I'm Emily Winter from WSMP-TV News. May I speak to Sam Terhune, please."

"I'm sorry, but Sam isn't taking calls."

"I see. To whom am I speaking?"

"Tina. Tina Terhune. I'm Sam's mom."

"I see. Is Sam there, Ms. Terhune? You said 'isn't taking calls.' Does that mean he's at home but refusing to speak to anyone?"

"Yes. Well, no. I mean, yes, he's here but no, he

won't talk. I've been trying to get him to eat something, get off the couch, read a book. Anything but just sitting there, staring off into space. He's said maybe two words since he got up and he looks terrible, like he got up so early because he couldn't sleep at all."

"Do you know if he's troubled about the NWCC bombing? Is there something about it which is causing his—Ms. Terhune, I don't mean to be forward, but what you're describing sounds like your son's depressed. Do you know why?"

"You don't have children, do you? No teens in your house?"

"No, no children."

"I thought so. Since Sam turned fifteen, he's been what you call 'depressed' as often as not. He's cranky, sullen, sarcastic, then he's utterly charming and delightful. Sometimes in the space of two minutes, Ms.—Winter, is it?"

"Yes. Emily Winter."

"He goes up and down like a yo-yo. What I'm trying to say is that our Sam isn't depressed, he's just another teenaged boy. I love him to pieces and he's fundamentally a good, solid person, but he can't leave for college soon enough to suit me. Oh, dear, you won't use that, will you?"

"No, of course not. The thing is, I spoke with him while he was on the picket line at the clinic and I'd like to ask a few more questions. Could you at least let him know I'm the one calling?'

"You spoke to him? I had no idea. Hold on."

Emily settled back in her chair, but Tina Terhune was back on the line in a matter of seconds.

"He's gone," she said.

"Gone?"

"He was on the couch when I came to answer the phone, but he's not there now. I called out, but I think he's gone for a walk or something. He's not here."

"I'm going to give you my number. Please ask him to call me when he comes back."

"Sure."

Tina Terhune took the number; Emily ended the call by punching the button on her phone so hard she broke a fingernail.

"This won't do," she said, "this simply will not do at all."

She sat perfectly still, her chin resting in her hands, her eyes closed until an idea floated before her. She stood up and walked out of the cubicle, snaking around several others to reach the elevator door. She entered and tapped the button marked Studio; when the doors didn't close immediately, she pushed the Close Doors button impatiently half a dozen times.

In the spacious studio from which WSMP broadcast all its news programs, Emily walked past the morning team's set—a desk from which news was delivered and an arrangement of couches and chairs which were meant to appear casual and comfortable—and the more formal and business-like evening news desk next to the morning set. Beyond both was a large empty blue screen and a tall bar stool with a pointer resting against it. This was Billy Hutchins' domain, the weather station; just beyond it sat a large, ornate desk. Next to the desk was a frame which held a garish cowboy saddle. Billy Hutchins himself was bent over an array of charts and maps.

"Billy?"

He looked up frowning but a big smile burst open when he saw her.

"Hey! It's my favorite reporter. How y'all doin'? What brings you down to my little spread here?"

His faint Southern draw and expansively open, friendly attitude made him a welcome guest in hundreds of thousands of homes every night, but beneath the aw-shucks façade lay a very crafty entertainer. Among his acquired skills, Billy Hutchins knew Chicago and its vast surrounding suburbs neighborhood by neighborhood, street by street. He knew neighborhood nicknames, he knew where all the schools were; he was a walking tour guide of Chicagoland and, every single night, Hutchins found a way to insert what he knew into his weathercasts. The crew who worked with him all knew that he kept a list of every city, town, village, and every neighborhood with a name on a clipboard. After each weather report, he checked off the places he'd mentioned and, in his next appearance, moved down the list. Eventually, everybody who watched knew that Billy Hutchins cared about them and their little corner of the world because he'd gone out of his way to mention that corner.

"Billy, I hear you have a crisscross phone directory."

"'Course I do, child. Straight up phone books for every suburb, too, and maps, I got maybe a hunnert of those. You need something?"

"I'm chasing down some folks we need to interview, but all I have are phone numbers for a couple of them. And their names, of course. But no addresses."

Billy stood and walked over to a set of filing cabinets behind his saddle. He pulled open a heavy drawer, peered in, said "Nope" and pulled open another. On the fourth try, he hefted a large book, returned to his desk and dropped it on an open corner. It sent a substantial breeze through everything else on his desk.

"Up to date," he said with a grin. "Be my guest."

Emily carried the book to an empty chair and pored through it. Eventually, she had secured street addresses associated with the phone numbers for Sam Terhune, Norman Brent and Jon Haskill's home and office.

On her way back to her desk, Emily tapped on Bert Presley's door.

"I'm not getting any response from the RTLC crowd," she said. "No answers, no return calls. So, I ran down home addresses for them. I've already been to Carol Lobes' home, so I had that one. Anyhow, I'm planning to run them down so I can get their reactions. Should I use Kern?"

"Yeah," said Presley, "but before you do that, follow up on this. I just got off the phone with her."

He handed her a note. It contained Alicia Good's office phone number and a message: "Ready when you are. Call or come to the office."

"Finally," said Emily, "I've been hitting brick walls all morning."

"She's eager to get to you, that one. She went through the main newsroom number and they told her you weren't at your desk. She asked them to put her through to me. Told me she knows you need an interview and didn't want to take any chances, so she called the boss. Grab Scott and go get it."

"Done."

Alicia Good had a small office in a small law firm. Kern couldn't get an angle which satisfied him, so they moved to a conference room and set up there.

"Ms. Good, I understand that the Northside Women's Care Clinic's board of directors met this morning. Can you tell us what happened in that meeting?"

"Yes. First, we want to express our deep sorrow at the loss of Dr. Joan Estrada. Dr. J was with us from the day NWCC was created—she helped us set up our clinic, she served hundreds of women who confronted all sorts of medical issues and she was, always, kind, thoughtful and compassionate. There is no doubt that she made her patients' lives better and she certainly saved many of those lives. Her loss will be felt by women and their families across Chicago.

"We condemn in the strongest possible terms the horrendous attack on our facility. We are convinced that this wanton violence is the result of a determined effort to deny women their right to control their bodies and their medical care. There can be no excuse for such hateful action and we demand that those responsible be exposed and brought to justice."

"Do you plan to resume your services and can you provide us with details about where and when that might occur?"

"We will offer the same full range of services and care we provided in our clinic before it was destroyed. We will do so as fast as we possibly can. We are already searching for a new location and we have requested our insurance provider to expedite the funds we'll need to restore everything we lost— and we lost everything—with the greatest possible speed. We are already contacting all our patients and counselling them, arranging for interim care until we are reestablished. Finally, we have created an endowment to help us come back stronger and more resolute. That fund will honor Dr. J and we hope the thousands she treated will help us continue her vital work."

Alicia paused and gathered herself. She looked directly into Scott Kern's camera.

"We will not be turned away from our mission. We will not stop providing health care to women and their families. Threats, intimidation and violence will not stop us. The Northside Women's Care Clinic is and will always be stronger than the hatred and bigotry we confront."

Alicia's anger and determination were so strong that Emily asked nothing more. She signaled Kern to douse the lights and turn off his camera. When the camera went off, Emily rose and walked over to Alicia.

The two women hugged.

"Was that okay?"

"No, Alicia, that was not 'okay.' That was stirring, inspirational, powerful and poignant. If that entire interview isn't included, verbatim, in tonight's broadcasts, I swear I'll quit on the spot."

Alicia laughed.

"Lord, don't do that! We aren't kidding about justice. We're working with the police, of course, but I told the board this morning that I was sure you'd be working on this story. We're depending on you. You can't quit because women all over this city need you."

"Thank you. I'm just doing my job, but I appreciate your recognition. But it seems clear to me that women need you and NWCC a lot more than they need me. Let me know if anything else breaks, okay?"

"You'll be the second to know," said Alicia. "Take care."

Two days later, Emily walked into Bert Presley's office.

"I'm going to the NWCC memorial service,"

she said. "I'll be out for the rest of the day. The editing bay has my stuff from the welfare fraud news conference this morning, it'll be ready for the six o'clock 'cast."

"You taking a crew?"

"Of course not."

"What, 'of course not?' It's a legit story, the bombing is still fresh in everybody's mind. It's not a top of the 'cast story anymore, but we could still—"

"No, Bert. Sorry. I don't think it's right, intruding on a private event which is devoted to grief. They didn't announce it, it wasn't on the City News budget—it's just their extended family."

"Of which you're a member?"

Emily nodded. "I'm close to a member of their board. She thought I might want to attend. She certainly doesn't expect me to show up with Scott and a camera. I think it would be rude, unseemly."

"But you'll keep an eye out for leads, maybe a fresh angle we can use?"

Emily sighed.

"Yes. You can take the girl out of the newsroom, but you can't take the newsroom—"

"Once a reporter, always a reporter," said Bert. "I get it. Okay, then, go. Keep your antenna up."

"Thanks. See you in the morning."

There were perhaps a hundred people in the pews of the North Shore Unitarian Church in Deerfield. Emily recognized the members of the NWCC staff, all seated in the second row on the left, and

Alicia Good who sat with Carmen Howorth in the front row. Although a warm luminescent light filtered through the beautiful stained glass windows, the room itself seemed somber.

Several members of the board, including Alicia, spoke, each in turn carrying the history of the clinic chronologically forward, charting Joan Estrada's determination, influence and guidance at each step. There were some light moments of humor, a couple centered on the diminutive doctor's delight in her nickname, but the tone of the ceremony was deeply infused with grief and, in several cases, sharp anger.

Carmen Howorth spoke not of her colleague's professional achievements but, instead, celebrated the friendship the two women had forged, alternating between the joy of that friendship and the pain of its loss. She concluded by introducing a young woman.

"In honoring the work to which Dr. J. devoted— and ultimately gave—her life, we wanted to share with you not only her significant accomplishments but the grace and compassion with which she approached her patients. As we thought about that aspect of Dr. J's remarkable life, one of her patients contacted us to ask if she might speak today. Her story so touched us that we invited her to join us today."

A young woman rose from her aisle seat and walked slowly to the lectern. She took a position beside the podium so she was fully exposed to the mourners.

"So many people think the decision to terminate a pregnancy is easy, that women who make that choice don't have any anguish or regrets. That is not true and nobody understood that better than Dr. J.

"When I came to her clinic, I was alone and frightened." The young woman paused, her eyes tearing, and took a deep breath. "I was the victim of a rape and I was pregnant. After he raped me, I fell apart. I couldn't control my own life and I sure wasn't ready to be a parent. I knew I couldn't have that baby, but people kept telling me I had to. There was nothing easy about it.

"Dr. J understood. She spent hours—literally hours—talking with me, sharing her heart with me, offering me her friendship, her love, her support. In the end, I made the choice I had to make. It wasn't easy and it sure wasn't comfortable, but it was the right choice. Dr. J. cared for me, truly cared, not just in a clinical way, but as a friend." Again, she fell back to gather herself and wipe her tears away. "Dr. J. enabled me to make my own choice and I am at peace with it. I hope Dr. J has peace now, too."

Chapter Ten

It was midafternoon when Scott Kern pulled up in front of Norman Brent's home in Evanston, half a block from the Skokie line. The apartment building had six units; the directory said Brent was in Unit F. Emily and Scott climbed three flights of stairs, Kern taking a couple of short breaks along the way.

Emily knocked on the door. Kern leaned his camera, his tripod and himself against the wall, huffing just enough to be heard. A few moments later, the peep hole in Brent's door slid open. Emily took a step back and held up her ID card.

"Emily Winter, Mr. Brent. WSMP-TV. May we come in and ask you some questions about the bombing at NWCC?"

The door did not open.

"I got nothing to say to you. Go away."

"It's important, sir. I'm sure you understand that, since your group was demonstrating near the clinic, people might suspect you had something to do with the bombing."

"I got nothing to say to you. Go away."

"Mr. Brent—"

The door flew open. Scott pushed away from the wall and picked up his camera.

"You can stand out there all night long, lady," said Brent, "it won't make any difference. I got nothing to say. Our Steering Committee has decided that we won't respond to anybody but the cops. No interviews, period."

"Mr. Brent, please—"

The door slammed shut.

"I don't believe that fellow wants to talk to you," said Kern.

"Not a smart strategy, Scott. He must know that I'm going to report their refusal to comment. That won't look good."

"Pretty clear he doesn't give a hoot about that, isn't it?"

"Yes," said Emily. "Let's run over to Elk Grove and see if Carol Lobes will give us something. Maybe she'll be more cooperative—she talked to me last time."

"Isn't she on that Steering Committee?"

"She's the co-chair."

"So, if they've decided—"

Emily caught and held Kern's eyes.

"I won't give up, Scott. It's a critical piece of the story. Maybe I can persuade her to open up, even if it's just for background."

"Fat chance," said Kern.

Emily's eyes softened.

"Oh, come on, Scott-so. Elk Grove's not that far,

what can it hurt to try?"

"You know it's almost four o'clock, right? We'll hit early rush hour traffic, this time of day. It'll be forty minutes before we get over there from here. Then we'll have to haul it to get back to the studio to get the interview with that babe—"

"Alicia Good, and I'm not nuts about 'babe.' You heard her—she's a dedicated professional doing important work. 'Babe' is sort of demeaning."

"Sheesh," said Scoot, "I didn't mean anything, Emily."

"I know. Sorry, I just get tired of—never mind. If we leave now, it'll take us twenty minutes to get to Lobes' place."

Kern made a face.

"Yeah, right. You wanna bet?"

"How much?"

"How about a pizza?"

"Deep dish? From Uno?"

"From Uno. Deep dish. Sausage."

"Done."

"One thing, Scott."

"What's that?"

"Play fair. No long way around, no 20 miles an hour. Straight there, posted limits."

"Hey, now I'm insulted. You think I'd do that just to win a bet?"

"Of course I do," she said, grinning, "that's why I'll be paying close attention all the way."

"I'm still gonna win," he said.

Carol Lobes did open her door to Emily, but only to say that she couldn't say anything about the bombing. Emily pressed her. Lobes repeated what Brent had said—no interview, no comment—and said she was in the middle of preparing dinner and gently closed the door on them.

Back at the studio, Emily and Scott edited the interview with Alicia Good and Emily prepped copy explaining that, despite several attempts, representatives of RTLC had refused to comment on the clinic bombing. When she was done, she let Presley and the evening news Director know the piece was ready and then, with Kern in tow, went to a desk where she dialed a number and placed the order: Deep dish, sausage. She asked for the cost and handed Kern the exact amount, with a tip for the driver.

"I'm going live to intro the Good piece, so I have to be in the studio. Save me a slice, okay?"

He grinned at her; she gave him a punch on the shoulder.

Just before noon the next day, the phone on her desk buzzed.

"Emily Winter."

"Hi, Emily, Kirstin Bonner here."

"Hi! How are you?"

"I'm fine, thanks. Listen, I've got something you may be able to use. Do you have a minute?"

"I may have, but you should know I'm about to faint from hunger. I skipped breakfast."

"You shouldn't do that. It's not good for you."

"Too busy. I got here early to go over all my notes. I'm not getting anywhere with the investigation. Then our planning session ran long. I couldn't stand eating out of the vending machines in the break room, so I'm close to famished."

"Well, then, let's meet for lunch."

"Where?"

"How about Tony G's? The pizza place in the loop, you know it?"

"I do," said Emily, "but I had a slice last night, don't want more today. How about the deli in the Mallers Building?"

"Of course," said Bonner. "Your all-time favorite. I can be there in ten minutes. I'll call ahead and order. You know what you want?"

"Tuna on rye, potato chips, please, no fries."

"Drink?"

"Coffee."

"Got it. I'll see you there."

They were just ahead of the lunch rush, so the sandwiches were ready when Bonner arrived; she was setting up at a quiet table as Emily walked in the door.

They hugged and Emily sat and downed half her sandwich before she leaned back to relax a bit.

"So," she said, "what's up?"

"I saw last night's news so I know you're covering the bombing. I may have a lead for you."

Emily sat up and leaned forward.

"What?"

"I just heard this and I haven't had time to confirm it or anything, but I was having a chat with our real estate guy. He mostly oversees sales and leases, but he also negotiates for sites Cary wants to buy. Lately, Cary's been itching to find some new properties."

"He doesn't have enough already? Seems to me every other building in the Loop is a Chase property."

"Well, we do have a lot going on downtown," said Kirsten, "but Cary wants diversity. He's interested in other parts of the city, smaller projects in neighborhoods that aren't hot yet but have a lot of potential. Larry, that's Larry Smith, the real estate guy, has the word out and he told me this morning that he got a call from somebody named Randy Hoffman."

"Who's he?"

"He owns a handful of storefronts, mostly near north. He heard Cary's in the market so he got in touch and said he's interested in unloading two or three of his holdings. He claims he's got a hot deal in the works, but he needs some upfront cash to make it work, so he wondered if Cary wants to snap them up."

"So?"

"So, one of the properties he's happy to unload is on Clark Street."

"Don't tell me—"

Bonner nodded emphatically.

"He owns the NWCC building. They had a five-year lease, just under three years remaining. He knows it's rubble, but he claims it's prime real estate and it wouldn't be hard to clear the lot and develop it. He says it's zoned so Cary could do retail on the ground floor and two or three stories of residential above it."

"Well, isn't that interesting!"

"I thought so. Here, I got all this from Smith."

Bonner slid a piece of Chase Enterprises letterhead across the table; it contained a typed list of the holdings Smith was offering, their current estimated value and Hoffman's contact information and office address.

Emily folded it neatly and dropped it in her satchel.

"How much was lunch?"

"We'll split it. You owe me—"

"You bet I do," said Emily, "this is the only lead I've got, so I'm picking up the tab. What was the total?"

Emily reimbursed her friend and chatted for just a few more minutes before she rose and left, eager to get to work.

Randy Hoffman was almost as round as he was tall. The chair behind his desk was oversized and he filled it; it sagged perceptibly when he sank into it after offering Emily a folding metal chair facing him across the desk.

"So, how can I help you? Winter, did you say? You in the market for a solid commercial property, I got a bundle you'll wanna give some serious consideration. Sharp long term investment."

"Winter is right, sir. Emily Winter, but I'm not in the market, I'm with WSMP, Team 8 News."

"You told me that, right? On the phone? I got so many balls in the air, I keep losin' track of stuff. What's the news got to do with me?"

"I understand that you own the building where the Northside Women's Care Clinic had their offices."

"Yeah. What a mess. Been tryin' to unload that one but nobody's gonna touch it now, the shape it's in. It's a stone-cold loser. Lousy break, but what are you gonna do, eh?"

"Have you filed an insurance claim?"

"Hell, yeah. I drove over there that same afternoon, the day the place got torched. Took one look and called my insurance guy, went straight to his office, filed a claim, total loss. The place is destroyed. You seen it?"

"Yes, I was there that morning. Before that, you were trying to sell that property?"

"I was. No offers and there sure as hell won't be any now. I had a deal lined up, gonna sell two, three of my properties and put it all into this great little mall, corner location, lots of parking, a rock-solid gas station facing the corner, generates strong rent every month, lease has six years to run. Cherry piece of land, cherry deal, too. The fire killed it. Probably could have pulled it off with what the insurance company's gonna shell out, maybe a short-term bridge loan to supplement their payment, but no dice now. You want some chocolate, sweetie?"

Hoffman pulled open a desk drawer and extracted a box of Frango Mints, a ceramic bowl filled with M&M'S and a plastic bag containing a variety of what were, unmistakably, Halloween candy bars.

"No, thank you. I just had lunch."

"So, you need dessert, right?"

"Really, Mr. Hoffman, thanks, but no thanks."

He picked through the mint box and made a couple of choices; while he consumed them, both in his mouth at the same time, he grabbed a handful of M&M'S.

"I want to be sure I understand you. You were planning to sell the NWCC building and use the proceeds to buy another property. The insurance money would be enough to complete your other deal but it's on hold. Is that right?"

"Yup, more or less. I was going to bundle a couple of other small properties into the deal, give me some breathing room."

"How long had the NWCC building been on the market?"

"I'd been shopping it around for, what, two, three months."

"While your other deal was still alive, right? That must have been frustrating."

"You bet your—oops, shouldn't say that in front of a lady, huh? Yes, there were others looking at the little mall, so I wanted to jump in early and grab it."

"But if you couldn't sell it, the insurance would have been just as good, right?"

"Close enough."

"If the investigator hadn't found evidence of arson, the insurance payment would have been a, well, a welcome influx of cash."

"Yeah, it would—hey, just a second here, lady. Are you thinkin' I torched the place myself?"

"How much money is involved?"

"A lot. Place was fully insured for replacement at current market rates. Exactly how much is none of your business."

"I imagine it's enough so the investigators who are working on the explosions could view it as a fairly compelling motive. I'd also like to know how you feel about the work being done in the clinic."

"What, I'm one of those pro-life zealots? Not this boy—I say live and let live. So, you *are* accusing me. I'll be damned. That's nuts. You think I don't know that arson's gonna screw up any settlement? I been in this bidness a long time, honey, I know all about riders and coverage exclusions, all that. You're right, I wanted to unload the place in a hurry, but that don't mean I smoked it when it wouldn't sell. They were payin' their rent, I had no beef with them. You're crazy."

"You said you went to the building the day it was fire bombed. When was the last time you were there before that?"

"You mean, did I happen to be in the 'hood around six o'clock that morning? C'mon, doll, I ain't that stupid. Besides, like I say, torchin' the place

only slowed everything down. I don't get nothin'
for who knows how long?"

Emily nodded. Hoffman's indignation seemed
genuine but she found it curious that he knew
exactly when the building had been attacked.

"Where were you? That morning, I mean."

"Home. Asleep."

"Alone?"

He snorted.

"Nah, I had a couple-a them bunnies, from the
club, with me. They couldn't get enough. Of course,
I was alone. Been sleepin' alone in a bed for two
ever since the old lady walked out."

"So, nobody to back up your story."

"Geez, baby, lay off, wouldja? Nobody needs
to back up my damn story. I didn't torch my own
place. You'd have to be an idiot, right? I mean, it's
the first place the cops'd look, right? You'd never
get away with it."

"So, you've talked to the police?"

"Not yet. Well, I confirmed I own the place over the
phone. I'm bettin' they're comin' 'round soon enough."

He yanked the plastic bag open and pulled out
two mini Musketeers.

"You sure you don't want something?"

"No, thanks."

"Okay, your loss. So, we done here, honey? I
got stuff I gotta do, you know, places to go, people
to see."

"Yes, I think I've got what I need. Thanks for

your time. We're still working on this story, but if we break it open, we may want to talk with you again. You'll be around?"

"Where else I gonna be?"

"Good to know. One more thing, if you don't mind."

He shrugged. "What?"

"I'm not your sweetie or your honey and I'm certainly not a baby or a doll. Thanks again for your time."

"Sure. You want an Almond Joy, take on the road with you?"

Emily smiled, shook her head and left.

Back in her cubicle, Emily reviewed her notes and then dialed the phone.

"Potter, homicide."

"Winter, 'SMP.'"

"Nails! What's up?"

"Time to do some trading. I have something, may be useful to you. I'll trade for anything you got."

"NWCC fire, right?"

"Right. You go first."

"That's easy—I don't have anything. "

"No new scientific stuff from the labs or Sheehan?"

"All quiet."

"Suspects?"

"Well, every so-called pro-life activist in town, of course. Probably only, what, a couple hundred thousand or so of them, greater Chicago?"

"Nobody specific? Lobes or Brent?"

"One of the other guys got in touch, says they both have good alibis."

"Anybody talked to Randy Hoffman?"

"The guy who owns the building? How do you know about—"

Emily laughed.

"Give me a little credit, Jack. I do have sources, you know. And maybe an instinct or two. Somebody told me he'd been trying to unload the building before it went up, I thought he might be a viable suspect."

"And?"

"And, I don't know. He's hungry to unload the property, no doubt about that. But, the fire did him more harm than good, at least in the short term—there's no way he's going to get an insurance settlement—"

"Until we close the case."

"Exactly. I also wondered if he had a beef with the women at the clinic, but I don't think so. On the other hand, I didn't tell him when the bombs went off, but he knew exactly when."

"Hardly a surprise, Nails. It was all over the news." He laughed. "You didn't hear about it?"

"Very funny. All in all, I'd say he's not a likely suspect."

"Sounds like you're right, but we'll reach out all the same."

"Good luck."

"Thanks."

She sat for a moment and then picked up her notepad to review what she'd written in the

Hoffman interview. She flipped the pages back, noting that Brent and Lobes had refused her and, as far as she knew, had said nothing publicly about the attack on NWCC. She wondered if perhaps Lobes had provided Brent's alibi, and vice versa, and made a note to check back with Potter about that. She glanced at her notes about Jon Haskill and Sam Terhune, saw nothing new and sighed.

She set about packing her satchel to leave when Daniel Malafronte walked up to her cubicle and knocked on one of the walls as if it were her door.

"Daniel," she said.

"May I come in?"

"Sure."

She cleared a pile of newspapers from the chair next to her desk. She wasn't sure how to react to his presence. It was odd, certainly, since the man had never dropped by before and he was hardly ever in the news room at all. It was a little unsettling as well. She and Bert Presley had not spoken of Malafronte's role in the story about his son-in-law's surveillance company, so she didn't know if Malfronte knew that she had flagged his transgression—was he here to chide, or perhaps berate, her?

"How can I help you, Daniel?"

"I've been meaning to talk to you, but we haven't crossed paths since I stopped coming to the morning planning sessions, so I figured I'd catch you before you left."

"Talk to me?"

Emily tensed and took a long breath.

"Not exactly. I want to apologize."

"For what?"

"I put you in a terrible position. Not you specifically, mind you—I didn't know Bert would assign you to the story about closed circuit security cameras, but that's what happened. Bert didn't say so, but I'd be very surprised if you weren't the one who found out about my connection to Bad Guy Eyes."

Emily blushed.

"Yes. I talked to a couple of their employees and a customer, but I wanted to find out how extensively these systems are being used and I figured the company—maybe one of their sales guys—could give me some good background."

"And you found my connection."

"Yes, I did."

"Good for you."

"Excuse me?"

"Good reporting and, once you saw the problem, good that you told Bert about it. I was out of line, of course. I didn't give it much thought at the time, but when Bert pointed out how it would appear, the head of the News Department planting stories about a business his family—well, I don't have to explain it to you. You knew."

"I've been struggling with some internal conflicts of my own lately, Daniel, so it was kind of on my mind anyhow. I wasn't sure how to deal with it, so I went to Bert."

"And that was the right thing to do. Now, I mean after the fact, I see how—I don't know, how bad it was. I'm embarrassed about that—V.P. for News should know better, right?"

"Well, now you do."

"Yes, indeed. I apologized to Bert as soon as he came to me about it, but you weren't there. He didn't tell me you went to him, by the way. He approached it as if he'd been the one to discover the link. After we agreed that we had to kill the story, I guessed that he'd assigned it to you. When I asked him about that, he dodged the question, so I figured I had it right. The point is, I put you in an awkward position and I want to tell you that I regret that and that it won't happen again. Ever."

"Thank you," said Emily. "Can I ask you a question?"

"Sure."

"Did Bert ban you from the morning meetings?"

"As punishment? He probably should have, but it was my idea."

"Really? Why?"

"Because I didn't think I belonged. Mistake like that, the whole news operation would have been compromised, so I told him I'd take a break. Using the extra time to give myself a crash course in journalism ethics."

"Really? How?"

Malafronte pulled a magazine out of his jacket pocket.

"*Chicago Journalism Review*. I subscribed and then I went to their offices and got their help finding articles about conflicts of interest. They're strong critics, but they're also honest and fair. I've got more to learn, but what they've given me is a good start."

"Well, I'm impressed," said Emily. "I know the *Review* guys. I see most of them at Riccardo's every Friday. I admire what they do. They hold our feet to the fire when we get it wrong, but that's because they want to make us better at what we do. Will you be coming back to our meetings?"

"When I'm ready," said Malafronte. "I want to be sure I'm not a liability. Soon, maybe, but time will tell."

"Well, I hope so. It's not quite the same without you in the room."

"Kind of you to say so. It looks to me like you're packing up to get out of here, Emily. I won't keep you any longer. Have a good evening."

"Thanks, Daniel. You too."

He left and when he was out of range, Emily said, "Well, now, isn't that something?"

Chapter Eleven

"I'm telling you," said Benjamin Winter, "it's a golden opportunity."

"Private practice?" said Greg Good. "You're out of your mind. I'd start out with absolutely no clients and it would take years to build a practice. Besides, I love what I'm doing."

Benjamin grinned.

"You'll have more clients than you can handle in no time. Surely you can see how, Greg. Billboards, bus benches, those ad banners on taxis, maybe even TV. 'When It Comes To The Law, Greg Is Really Good.'"

"What on earth are you two talking about?" Emily looked as confused as she felt.

They were sitting on two blankets on the lawn at the Ravinia Festival, awaiting a concert by the Chicago Symphony Orchestra. The outdoor venue was crowded with picnickers and their baskets; the air was still and damp, the temperature backing down from its peak just shy of 90 degrees and it seemed, at least to Emily, that it was somehow cooler in suburban Highland Park than it had been in the city when they'd all piled into Greg's bright red Ford Pinto for the excursion.

"The Supreme Court has approved lawyers advertising," said Ben, waving a drumstick in the air. "I have not the slightest doubt that my friend can take full advantage of that decision. 'Greg's a Good lawyer.' 'Need legal help? Get somebody Good.' 'You deserve a Good lawyer.' I see wealth and prosperity in his immediate future."

Greg laughed.

"You could do the same thing, my friend. Leave your firm, go out on your own. 'Winter is a winner.' No, 'Winner Winter' is better. Or maybe 'In trouble? Get the lawyer who's as tough as a Chicago Winter.'"

"Greg and I could go into practice together," said Alicia. "We'd be the Good Law Firm. Or Greg and Ben could open a firm. You'd be the only place in town which could honestly guarantee everybody Good Winter."

Greg said "Good one."

Ben groaned in mock horror.

"You're all being silly," said Emily, "and you're making me nervous. Greg belongs at ACLU—he's perfectly suited to that position and their mission. Alicia loves the little firm she's in, right? They respect her work and she has a good income. And, speaking of income, Ben and I wouldn't last a month on my salary while he's out trying to hustle business—Herberger, Whittier Stineford & Bovie may elevate him to partner soon and, believe me, we need that paycheck. I think you're all exactly where you belong."

"Ah, m'love," said Benjamin, "'tis mere speculation, however amusing. While I admit I've been musing about it since the ruling, I daresay Greg is no more likely to leave his position than I am to leave mine. Excellent chicken, by the bye. Superior repast, Ms. Good."

"Thank you, sir. I swiped the recipe from Greg's mom. Emily, pour me another glass of wine and tell me what's going on with the NWCC investigation."

"Not enough. The two folks who run RTLC won't talk to me. Neither will a fellow who appears to be their sugar daddy. I've connected with a kid who was one of the demonstrators and we're going to talk, but I don't think he's up to arson, never mind murder. I spoke with my homicide contact and he says they've got three detectives working on the case but they haven't gotten any further than they were when the arson and coroner's reports came in."

"That's discouraging," said Alicia. "I'd hate to think whoever did this is going to get away with it. That's just not right."

Ben said, "Dr. King asserts that the arc of history bends slowly but it bends toward justice. There are a lot of people who are demanding that the arsonist be made to answer for his transgressions and more than a few of them can bring some pressure to bear—Aldermen, women's groups and such. I doubt the police will give up until they've produced salutary results."

"And Emily is still on the case," said Alicia, "and we all know she isn't easily deterred from doing her job."

"I can vouch for that," said Ben. "Anybody going to finish this potato salad or can I have it?"

They all shook their heads and Emily passed the container to him.

"Leave me one bite," she said. "After that, I want dessert."

———————

Max Winter swiveled around in his seat.

"We'll need some kind of signal," he said.

"For what?"

"I drop you off, you meet this kid, something goes wrong. I'm gonna swing the cab around so I can watch you meet up with him. You need help, we'll need some kind of signal."

"Max, he's just a kid. I don't think there's anything to worry about. I'm just going to ask him some questions. Besides, he's the one who called me. He said he wants to talk, that's all."

"Yeah. Well, I'm still gonna hang close by until I get a signal."

Emily shook her head.

"You're one tough customer, Max. Okay, how about this—you know how, at the end of every show, Carol Burnett—"

"Tugs on her ear! Perfect."

"As soon as I'm sure this kid isn't going to be a problem, I'll pull on one ear and you can go back to work. Okay?"

"Okay."

Emily climbed out of the cab and quietly groaned. It was not particularly hot—she guessed mid-seventies—but the humidity was so thick that it felt like a woolen blanket. She immediately regretted her decision to wear a long-sleeved blouse; it wilted when the moisture closed in on her and by the time she walked across the lawn to Buckingham Fountain, it was clinging uncomfortably to her body.

Sam Terhune—in shorts and a tee shirt—was sitting on the edge of the fountain wall. He was holding a cone-like cup with flavored purple shaved ice.

"Hello," said Emily.

"Hey. Thanks for meeting me."

"Sure. That looks good."

He smiled.

"Tastes like bad grape juice, but it's cold."

A breeze came up and some mist from the fountain blew in their direction. The extra moisture clung to them and Emily groaned again.

"I hope there's a good reason to meet here," she said. "I do love this city, but days like this make me love it a lot less."

"I'm leaving for UConn this weekend," said Terhune. "I'm going to Storrs early, probably find a job if I'm lucky, hang around the campus until it's time to register. I'm ready to leave."

He sounded both sad and excited.

"So, you said you wanted to talk. What about?"

He took a mouthful of ice and looked across the park to the lake.

"This is one of my favorite places. When I was a kid, we used to come here and my dad would let me climb over the wall and walk around in the water. It was like having a swimming pool. Then he and mom split and she had to work all the time so we didn't get to come here. I couldn't wait until I was old enough to go out on my own. I'd take a bus down here. I'm too old to get in the water, but I still love this fountain. Since I'm leaving town, I wanted to have one more visit."

Emily tugged on her earlobe.

"That's nice," she said, "but, you didn't answer my question."

He turned to face her.

"I wanted to apologize for ducking you when you called. I should have talked to you, but I just didn't want to. I was too upset."

"About the bombing?"

He winced.

"Yeah. I felt terrible about that, especially when I heard that lady got killed. I don't like what they do at that place, but burning it down? That's not right."

There was something in his manner, an edge, a hint of guilt. Emily hesitated, deciding how to approach him.

"Do you know anything about it?"

"No, just that it was wrong. I mean, it's okay to picket and all that, let them know there are people who think what they're doing is wrong, maybe even make it harder for them to do what they do—"

He stopped and hung his head, his ill-ease was still more evident.

"Any idea who's responsible for the bombing?"

He flinched.

"No."

"Something's bothering you, Sam. Tell me."

His gaze went back to the lake. Emily waited.

"Did you have something. . .are you somehow responsible?"

He shook his head.

"Not exactly."

He met her eyes and she saw his anguish. She considered and, after a pause, an idea struck her.

"Red paint," she said.

His shoulders drooped, a ragged sigh escaped and his nod was subtle but unmistakable.

"You splattered red paint on the building."

"Yes. How'd you know?"

"An educated guess."

"Good one. I was so angry about what they did, but it didn't feel like just standing around on the sidewalk was enough, you know? I mean, women kept going in there, we weren't making a difference."

"So you did something more than picket."

"Yeah."

"That's vandalism, you know."

"I do. I feel bad about it, wish I hadn't done it. I'm afraid—"

"You think damaging the building led to the bombing?"

"I don't know. Maybe."

"Did you smash a car window in their parking lot?"

"No." He shook his head emphatically. "I heard about it, it happened after I threw the paint, so maybe—"

"Maybe you upped the ante. Showed somebody else that more drastic action was okay."

"God, I hope not, but yeah, maybe somebody figured if it's okay to throw paint, it's okay to break windows or—"

He trailed off.

"Or throw a fire bomb."

"Yeah."

"But that wasn't you."

"Hell, no. Even if that woman hadn't died in there, that would be—I couldn't do anything like that."

He turned and watched a couple of kids leaning over the edge, splashing each other.

"You gonna turn me in?"

Emily smiled.

"Given what's happened since, I don't see much point in it."

"Thanks. Anyhow, I just want to get out of here, get away from all of it."

"I understand."

"There's one more thing."

"What?"

"I wanted to thank you."

"For what?"

"For calling the house."

"Why? I was just doing my job."

He shook his head.

"Mom didn't know."

Emily reached over the wall and let her hand dangle in the water; it felt good to have a wrist cool off. She used the moment to consider what he'd said.

"Your mom didn't—oh, I see. You hadn't told her about your girlfriend and the abortion."

Sam nodded.

"I just couldn't find a way, you know? I figured she'd be angry or disappointed in me, but either way, I didn't know how to talk to her about it."

"So when I called—"

"She wanted to know what it was all about and I told her that I'd been picketing down there. Told her why, too. She was disappointed. Still is, but she also understands and she said the abortion was the best thing for us, for me, anyhow. We had a good talk and she's the one who suggested I leave early, put all this behind me and move on."

"I'm sorry," said Emily. "I admit, it never occurred to me that I was giving something away. I didn't even think about that."

Sam finished his ice cup and stood up.

"It's okay," he said. "It's all good now. So, I gotta go, I got laundry to do and then I gotta pack and all. I just wanted to let you know I felt bad about ducking you and, like I say, I wanted to thank you for getting me to talk to mom. I was really pissed when you called the house, but it turned out to be a good thing. Thanks."

"I'm glad it worked out," said Emily. "Good luck."

They shook hands and Sam walked away. There wasn't a bounce in his step, but he did seem comfortable.

Emily sat and watched the fountain flow. When she finally rose to leave, a thought emerged which seemed almost as heavy as the humid air dogging her steps.

"I wonder," she thought, "if throwing paint was the end or just the beginning."

Chapter Twelve

The morning staff meeting was about to end when Emily spoke up.

"I called the press office at the cop shop yesterday," she said. "Nobody would talk to me. They said the only one over there who's allowed to speak about the investigation is Gary Easton. I left a message for him and then called back twice during the day. He isn't responding."

"So, we've got nothing new."

"Zip," said Emily. "Brent and Lobes won't cooperate, I still haven't heard anything from Jon Haskill—I've left him maybe a dozen messages. It's stagnant."

"I have an idea," said Nikki Stone.

"Shoot," said Presley.

"Emily could take a camera guy and stake out the office where this guy, the one who supposedly puts up RTLC's money, works. They stake the place out and as soon as he shows, Emily catches up to him and starts asking questions while the camera's rolling."

"That won't get us anywhere," said Emily. "All he'll do is dodge us or say 'No Comment.' That isn't news. It'd just be a waste of time."

"It would put pressure on him," said Nikki. "I saw a crew in L.A. do this, they caught up with a guy, a suspect in an embezzlement scheme, who didn't want to talk to them; the crew kept shooting while he tried to hide his face until he could get in the building. The footage was pretty exciting, the reporter and the camera guy chasing him across the parking lot and right up to the doorstep. He never said anything, but they ran the footage with the guy looking like he'd been caught red-handed. Everybody who saw it figured he had something to hide."

"Did he?" Emily leveled a wary eye at Stone.

"Well, no. He issued a statement the next day, denying any wrong-doing and his attorney chimed in, said they could prove he was innocent."

"Then it never should have aired. The poor guy lives with suspicion and doubt while the station airs a piece of film which is misleading and doesn't contain a lick of news, just to get a cheap chase on the air. That's not reporting, it's grandstanding."

Stone looked peeved.

"But, what if he breaks down? On camera, no less."

"Haskill? He won't," said Emily. "He's made it clear he has nothing to say."

"True," said Bert, "but there might be something there. What if you stake him out, but without a camera? Wait for him, talk to him, show him you're serious about covering the story."

"I'm skeptical, Bert. Besides, I can do that just

by calling him again.'"

"But, you're stuck, right? What else do you have to work with? Nothing, is what. Why not give it a go, see if you can shake something loose?"

"Okay, but no camera. I won't subject the man to that kind of empty exposure."

"No camera," said Bert. "That sort of thing isn't really our style anyhow."

Jon Haskill's company was south of the Loop, not far from McCormick Place. The area was mostly occupied by auto repair shops and other small businesses, so Haskill's building stood apart, newer and taller and sleeker than its neighbors. The building seemed to be bragging.

Uncle Max circled the block once before he pulled up to the curb near the building's parking lot entrance.

"Just like we did at the Park, with that kid," said Max. "I'm going to park across the street there, where I can see into the parking lot. Anything goes wrong, you give me a high sign or holler, okay?"

"Okay, Max, but we're wasting your time. Probably mine, too. He's not going to talk to me and we'll be headed back to the studio as soon as he shuts me down."

Max checked his watch.

"Almost noon," he said. "No place to walk to 'round here, grab a bite, he'll probably have to drive if he's gonna eat. See if those spaces are reserved, find out which one is his."

"I was planning to do just that," said Emily, "but thanks for the tip."

"No prob'. You ask me, it's gonna be that cream Caddy, parked closest to the entrance."

Emily smiled when she saw "Haskill" stenciled on the curb in front of the Cadillac; she started to give Max a thumbs-up and then realized that he might take it as a call for help. She walked over to the building's entrance. The lettering on the door said Consolidated Container Company and there was a buzzer beside the door. Emily thought about ringing the bell, but she suspected that doing so would just warn Haskill that she was there; forewarned, he'd just stay inside until she gave up and left.

It was a comfortable day. There was a light breeze coming off the lake and the sun was warm. Emily leaned against the building wall, keeping an eye on the Cadillac and leafing through her notepad. After half an hour, she was ready to either ring the doorbell or climb into Max's cab and give it up when a man in a suit, the jacket draped over one shoulder, came out. He swung the jacket around and fished into a pocket, extracting a set of keys. When he walked to the door of the Cadillac, Emily moved to meet him.

"Mr. Haskill?"

"Yes. Who are you?"

She held up her ID.

"Emily Winter, WSMP News. I'd like to ask you—"

"This is private property, ma'am. You have no

business here. Leave or I'll call the police."

"Sir, please, give me a moment, just a moment. I'm told you make substantial donations to Right to Life Chicago. Is that true?"

"No comment. I'm telling you, leave now."

"Do you know anything about the bombing of the Northside Women's Care Clinic?"

Haskill inserted his key and opened the door to his car.

"No comment."

He climbed in and shut the door, making a show of pushing down the lock button. He cracked the window just enough to show her a menacing glare.

"You come near me again, lady, and I'm going to call the cops and my lawyer. Watch your feet, I don't want to drive over your toes."

He started the car, put it in reverse and backed out quickly, cutting the wheel so sharply that Emily jumped back to avoid being brushed.

As the Cadillac moved toward the exit, Max palmed his steering wheel hard left and hit the gas hard. He came to a stop directly in front of the parking lot exit. Haskill slammed his brakes and laid on his horn.

Max jumped bolted out of the cab, heading for Haskill. Emily saw him and stepped forward.

"Max, don't."

Max ignored her, leaning in.

"You wanna be a tough guy, pal? Climb outta that boat."

"Max, stop it. Please. Leave him alone."

Haskill hit a button and his window closed completely. Max, his fists clenched and his face red, stood stock still, waiting.

Emily walked straight to the cab and pulled the door open.

"We're leaving now, Max. Let's go."

She climbed in and pulled the door shut.

"Now, Max. Let's go."

Max leaned in and raised his right fist.

"Threaten her again and we'll do more than talk, buddy."

Max backed away, keeping an eye on the Cadillac. He walked around his cab, pulled the door open, pounded a fist on the roof and pointed at Haskill. He slammed his door shut and pulled forward just enough to allow the Cadillac to nose out of the driveway.

"You want I should follow him, Emmy?"

"Absolutely not," she said. "Let him go all the way down the block before you move an inch."

Haskill sped down the street and turned at the corner.

"Max, you can't be doing stuff like that."

"That jerk tried to hit you. You think I'm gonna stand by and—"

"Max, take it easy. It was my fault, too—I was standing too close to his car. Besides, he didn't hit me and I don't think he was trying to. He just wanted to get away."

"You were in danger. That's all I saw."

"Max, listen to me, okay? First, that man's about

a foot taller than you are and he's got to be, what, ten, fifteen years younger? Plus, he's not wrong—he doesn't have to talk to me and I confronted him on his own property."

"Yeah, well—"

"No, Max. Listen to me. What happens if he's got your cab number or maybe remembers the plate number? He calls your boss, complains that you're harassing him, threatening him. You could lose your cab, maybe even your hack license. Then where would you be?"

Max pulled away from the curb, glancing at her as he did.

"You got a point there. Probably shoulda thought about that. Probably shoulda let it be, too, once I saw he hadn't hit you, but, you know—I won't let anything happen to you."

"I understand, Max, and I'm grateful that you care, but, there's one more thing."

"What's that?"

"If he calls my boss, tells him I'm using some crazy guy who threatens people when they won't talk to me, I'll be in a whole lot of trouble."

Max shook his head.

"Didn't think about that, either. Sorry. So, you want I should come into the station with you, tell your boss it was my mistake, you had nothin' to do with it? Get you off the hook?"

"Maybe later," said Emily, "but I don't think we need to go that far, at least not yet. I bet he wants nothing more to do with me, the station, any of it. If he complains, I'll decide if I need you to talk with Bert. Until then, let's just leave it alone, okay?"

"Okay. Back to the studio?"

"Yes."

"You had lunch yet?"

"Nope."

"Wanna grab a bite?"

"No, thanks."

"Okay."

Max drove carefully, and in silence. Emily turned away from him, watching the city roll by and collecting her slightly frazzled nerves.

When Max pulled into the circular drive and Emily swung the door open, Max leaned across the seat and tugged on her sleeve.

"Yes?"

"Just tell me this, okay? You think I put the fear of God in him?"

Emily laughed.

"No doubt about that," she said, "you certainly scared me. He's probably going to be looking over his shoulder for the rest of the week."

"He'd be nuts not to," said Max.

———————

"The file is fat. It'll take a long time to go through them all," said Carmen Howorth.

"That's okay," said Emily. "I'm not getting any-where with this story and the homicide detectives haven't made any progress either, so I might as well take a crack at this. Maybe it will shake something loose."

The two were in Howorth's apartment, sitting in a small bedroom which Howorth had converted into a home office. She leaned over and pulled a file cabinet open, extracting a thick folder.

"I keep these here so nobody else has to deal with them. At the clinic, I mean. There's some pretty ugly stuff here and I decided that it would make the staff even more uncomfortable if they saw these. They endure enough as it is."

She handed the folder to Emily. On the file tab, neat printed letters said "Fan Club." Emily laughed when she saw it.

"Gallows humor?"

Howorth smiled.

"Helps take the edge off. I've got some calls to make, but I can do that in the kitchen. You can sit in here. You want some coffee?"

"No, thank you. Have the police seen these?"

"A nice detective, Jack something. . ."

"Potter?"

"That's him. Seemed like a good man. Good looking, too. He asked the same question you did—had anybody threatened us—and I showed him the file. He spent a little time with it, but he didn't take any of them. He may have taken a note or two, but I don't think he found them useful."

Emily sighed. Potter's sharp instincts would have

identified a viable suspect among the hate mail, which meant her search would likely be a waste of time. But she had the file in front of her and no other leads to follow, so she thought maybe, just maybe, she'd see something he'd missed even as she had serious doubts.

Well over half of the hate mail was anonymous. More than a few featured words cut from newspapers and pasted on stationery. In the main, the mail fell into two categories—biblical quotations coupled with promises of eternal damnation or secular outrage at the clinic's mission. A few mentioned either Estrada or Howorth by name; one was a long and angry complaint about Sharon Anderson, the clinic's counselor who, the writer alleged, was insensitive and mean.

Emily sat on a small sofa and laid the mail out in piles on the floor. She set all the anonymous letters in a tall pile—no names meant no lead to follow. She separated all those containing no obvious threat into one pile and those containing benign threats—'God will punish you' 'You'll burn in hell'—in another. When she was done, she had a short stack of letters which were signed and contained enough menace to merit a second look. She was looking those over when Carmen came back.

"We may have found a new location," she said, smiling.

"That's good news," said Emily.

"It certainly is. Did you find anything? I mean, other than the fact that a lot of people don't think much of our little enterprise?"

"I doubt it," said Emily, "but I do have a question for you."

"Okay."

"Who is Gayle Bionni?"

Howorth raised her eyebrows.

"Huh, I'd forgotten about those. She's a former employee. She was our first fundraiser. She'd been with a foundation which supports families of children with cancer. She'd done quite well with them, but she couldn't get any traction for us. She never seemed comfortable selling our story—it's a lot more nuanced and difficult than sick kids—and we, that's Dr. J and I, decided that it just wasn't a good fit. We asked her to leave and she wasn't happy about that."

"Her letters are quite angry."

"She was quite angry with us, at least at first."

"She wrote three letters to you, all in the same month. What happened after that?"

"She got a job. At an animal shelter in Waukegan, I think, and the letters stopped."

"One of her letters says she plans to 'make you pay dearly.' Was she going to sue you or did she mean something more drastic?"

"She didn't sue us. Dr. J wrote her a pretty decent recommendation—ever the kind one, right?—so we figured somebody told her she didn't have much of a leg to stand on in court. And, as I said, the letters stopped."

"When did all this happen?"

"Earlier this year. We let her go in February,

I think."

"So, recently enough that she might still be angry? Agitated?"

"I suppose so."

"Do you have contact information for her? Any idea how I can reach her?"

"I think her new job is at something called Pet Paradise. As I said, it's in Waukegan."

"I can look it up. So, what about phone calls? Did you get threats over the phone?"

"A few. Mostly, we got prank calls, people who'd call a dozen times and hang up when we answered, that sort of thing."

"What about the threats? Anything you took seriously enough to, for example, call the cops?"

Howorth shook her head.

"Truth is, we were all so busy just keeping the place open and doing our jobs that threats were just an annoyance. Sometimes, we laughed at them 'cause they were so absurd—one caller said he was going to hammer our doors shut so we could never leave, stuff like that. Now, after Dr. J, after the fire, I wonder if we should have taken it all more seriously."

"How could you?" said Emily, gesturing at the stacks of paper on the floor. "Among all the empty threats, which one might be real? There's no way to know, is there? Plus, of course, it's far more likely that whoever threw those Molotov cocktails wouldn't warn you in the first place—sending you a letter or calling with a threat that specific would be too risky, wouldn't it? I don't see how you and your staff are at fault. None of you torched the building, after all."

"That's true," said Carmen. "Still—"

Emily waved her off.

"No. The person who attacked the clinic is responsible for that attack. Nobody else is."

"Maybe someday we'll know who that is."

"That's my intention," said Emily. "How were these organized before I spread them out? I'll put them back in order for you—by year, by date of arrival?"

Howorth smiled.

"No need. They were probably in order of receipt, but who cares one way or the other? Just stuff 'em back in the folder."

Emily did, taking brief notes about Gayle Bionni's letters.

"Thanks so much. I think Potter was right, there's nothing here. I'll check on Bionni just to be sure. Can I use your phone?"

"Sure."

Emily handed over the file folder and moved to the phone on the small desk.

"You free, Max? I need a ride back to the studio if you're available."

"Where you at?"

Emily gave him the address.

"I'm home. Oh, wait, you knew that, right, it's the number you called. Anyhow, I'm finishing lunch. Havin' a hot dog today, you know, the ones they serve at Wrigley. Couple more bites, I'm on my way."

They were close to WSMP's studios, turning into the circular driveway when the bullet shattered the passenger window.

At first, Emily wasn't sure what had happened. She heard the front window explode and saw the glass fly across the cab toward Uncle Max; it happened so quickly that she was confused, thinking that somehow she heard the shot after the glass broke.

Max screeched to a halt and swore, pitching himself sideways on the front seat.

"Duck, Emmy. Get down on the floor!"

She hesitated and Max shouted, "Now!" She slid off her seat and down. Everything grew silent.

"You okay?"

"I'm fine, Max. You?"

"Think I'm okay, too. You stay down, I'm gonna have a look."

"Don't."

He ignored her, raising up just high enough to peer out the broken window.

"I don't see anything," he said. "I'm gonna throw her in gear and whip up the drive. When I say so, you run—and I mean as fast as you can go. Go into the building, stay away from the door when you get in."

"Max—"

"Ready?"

The cab sped forward and slammed to a halt.

"Go!"

Emily bolted for the station's front door. Inside, she raced to the receptionist's counter and shouted.

"Call the police, tell them there's been a shooting."

The stunned receptionist froze.

"Now!"

Emily turned and went back to the door. Max was standing next to his cab, bent below the roof line, his eyes sweeping the area.

"Max, get in here."

Max didn't move.

"Max, run."

He dashed around the car and ran through the doors.

"Bastard broke my window," he said. "You sure you're okay?"

"I'm fine," said Emily. She reached out and took his arm and felt something sticky.

"Max, you're hurt."

"Nah. Little glass is all. Just a cut. Probably ruined this shirt, though."

Bert Presley and several others appeared; a security guard moved to the front door, talking on his radio.

"What the hell?" said Presley.

"Somebody shot at us," said Max.

"Are you hurt?"

"No."

"Me either," said Emily. As she spoke, she felt her knees give way and she sagged toward the floor.

Max caught her and led her to a couch. She sank into the cushions.

One of the newsroom crew found a first aid kit and used a scissors to cut Max's shirt sleeve away. He gently extracted several shards of glass and taped a bandage to the cuts.

"That hurt?"

"Nah."

Max walked over to Emily and sat beside her.

"You sure you're okay?"

Emily gathered herself and looked directly at him.

"I'm fine," she said and then she smiled.

"Something funny about this?"

"Not exactly, Max."

"What, then?"

"Don't you see? If somebody's shooting at me, there has to be a reason."

"I don't get it."

"I must be a threat to somebody, Max. Somebody doesn't want me doing my job."

"Yeah? So?"

"So, I must be doing my job. Somebody thinks I know something."

"Do you?"

"That's the funny part. I don't have the faintest idea what I know."

"You're in one wacky business, Emily Winter."

Chapter Thirteen

"I want you to call Jack Potter," said Benjamin.

"It's too late," said Emily, "it's nearly seven. Why would I call him?"

"It isn't obvious? Somebody tried to kill you."

"But they didn't. Jack's a homicide detective. There wasn't one."

"Of no consequence whatsoever, m'love. Had Max not been turning into the driveway, had you been in the front seat instead of in back, had the perpetrator been a better marksman—you do see, don't you, that you're in peril? It was only good fortune that you weren't hit. Or killed. Steps must be taken."

"I understand your concern, but that still doesn't mean I should call Jack. It's just not his territory. Besides, the patrol car showed up quickly and the two cops searched the area. They thought the shot came from the parking lot next door to our building, but they didn't find anything. They gave me a card, said I should call if anything else happened. I still have it. If something else happens, I'll call them. I promise."

Ben set his fork aside and stared at her.

"Not good enough. I want Potter to know of this so that he can spread the word among his colleagues and, perhaps, the culprit can be identified. Second, and of far greater import from my perspective, Jack will know who's best suited to protect you."

"Protect me?"

"Am I that obtuse? You need a bodyguard. I want you to have security until your investigation is concluded."

"That's absurd."

"It may well be, but that only enhances my determination. It is absurd that someone is foolish enough to shoot at you, but they may well be foolish enough to try again. I want you to be protected. I insist, Emily. If you won't seek assistance from Detective Potter, I shall pursue the matter on my own."

"How on earth can I do my job with somebody tagging along all the time? When I interview people, it's one-on-one. I get good material because I can listen and concentrate and the subject can concentrate on me. If there's somebody with me, somebody menacing and presumably armed, that's a problem. It destroys the intimacy."

Ben frowned and then leaned forward.

"A successful assassination would make an interview unproductive, too. We can find someone who knows how to be subtle but effective."

His tone and closeness told her that she wasn't going to dissuade him. She nodded.

"I'll call Jack tomorrow morning."

"Before I leave, please," said Ben. "I want to know what he says and what steps he recommends."

"There's no need—"

"Don't be daft, Emily. I'll not rest until I have full faith and confidence that you are under the scrutiny of the best available. We're not just protecting you here, you know."

"No?"

"No, m'love. We are protecting everything in my life worth having and holding. I intend to be completely and unabashedly selfish on that score."

———————

"Emily, Ben," said Jack Potter, "meet Karen Beth Constantine. Karen, Emily and Ben Winter."

The young woman smiled and extended her hand. Emily took it and smiled; Ben shook as well, focusing on the way she moved and the strength of her grip. He also noticed that, while she was in civilian clothes, she was wearing her equipment belt; it carried a holster and gun, a leather pouch with handcuffs and, dangling from a silver ring, a black baton.

"A pleasure to meet you both," she said. "The guys all call me K.B."

"Except the ones who call her less flattering names," said Potter with a wry smile.

Constantine smiled too. She was nearly a foot taller than Emily, slender and graceful with an athlete's body. Her smile was genuine and warm.

"There are a few of those," she said.

"Your qualifications, ma'am? For obvious reasons, Emily's safety and security are paramount. We want nothing less than the best."

"Of course," said Karen. "I joined the force five years ago. When they finally allowed women to wear the uniform, in '74, I was one of the first who went on patrol. I passed all their tests, held my own with the guys, took extra training in self-defense. I can handle a weapon pretty well, too."

"Last time the department staged a shoot-off," said Potter, "K.B. came in second."

"True," said Constantine. "Lost by two points."

Ben nodded. "And prior to joining the force?"

"Well, school, mostly. I graduated from U.C. Berkeley, major in criminal justice, minor in sociology. I ran for the women's track team, middle distances and relays. When I graduated, I was recruited by the California Highway Patrol and it seemed like a good deal so I signed up."

"What brought you to Chicago?" asked Emily.

"Family. My mom lives in Evanston and when Dad died, she didn't want to leave the house. I decided to come home so she'd have someone watching over her. We spent a little money to convert her garage into an apartment so I'm right there if she needs me but I have my own place."

"What are your hours?" Ben was taking notes.

"My hours?"

"Yes. There will be times when your job requires your presence, yes? We need to figure out how to cover those gaps."

Emily, at his side, gently tugged on his sleeve.

"Ben is on edge lately," she said. "Otherwise, I'm sure he would have invited you in. Please, join us in the living room. Would you like some coffee? A soft drink?

"Thank you," said K.B. "I just had my fourth cup and that's enough for—my goodness, the lake is practically in your living room. What a view."

"It's why we emptied our savings account," said Emily. "We used to rent here. When they converted to condos, we couldn't say 'No.' We had a little windfall and we poured every penny of it into this. I imagine we'll be here for a long time."

"Which is why we wish to retain your services," said Ben. "We want Emily to enjoy our home—and that view—for decades yet to unfold. She works days, Ms. Constantine—nine to five or six, sometimes earlier, sometimes later. I ask after your hours because I sincerely doubt that your duties will accommodate such a schedule plus, truth be told, we have no idea how long your services will be required. The assignment is open-ended."

"I understand," she said, "may I ask a question or two?"

"Please do."

"This incident, the shooting, is somehow tied to your work?"

Ben started to answer. Emily cut him off with a raised hand.

"That seems the only logical reason. Nothing else I'm working on is controversial, at least not in any way which would cause somebody to turn deadly. I have no idea how much longer it will take to find the person who bombed NWCC."

Constantine turned to Ben.

"Detective Potter says you want your wife protected. Do you also want me to find out who fired at her?"

"No, it's not an investigation. I trust others on the force will explore that aspect. As far as I'm concerned, your only task will be ensuring Emily's personal security."

"Then I can handle it," said K.B., "if your wife approves, of course."

"How?" There was an edge in Ben's voice.

"How, what?"

"You're on the job. How can you protect her when you're on patrol?"

"I won't be."

"I don't understand," said Ben. He turned to Potter. "I thought you said she is on the force."

Jack Potter shrugged.

"She is a member of the department," said Potter, "currently on paid leave."

Ben frowned deeply, turning back to K.B.

"What for?"

"Speaking up," said K.B. "When I arrived, Eighteenth District, that's near North, there were eight boxes of sanitary napkins stacked up in front of my locker. The nameplate on the locker said 'Bitch.' I smiled and mostly laughed it off and then I made a point of showing them that I'm as good a cop as they are. I went the extra mile, took double shifts so somebody could go to a kid's birthday party or take the family on a weekend trip, went out of my way to talk to them, be friends with them, knock back some beers after the shift. I did all I could to fit in."

"Go on," said Ben.

"It worked for most, but there are still two, maybe three guys who won't quit. They glued my locker shut, they stuck some pretty ugly signs on the bulletin board. The last straw, a week ago, I opened my locker and somebody had squirted bleach into those little louvers, the ones to let some air in. My uniform was ruined and I had to replace it, plus, I couldn't go on patrol that day 'cause I didn't have a backup, so the brass was not happy. Between the cost of a new uni and pissing off my sergeant, I decided it was time to put an end to it."

Ben nodded.

"I'm familiar with such shenanigans," he said, taking Emily's hand. "Emily has often encountered similar mistreatment. What did you do?"

"I filed a complaint. As soon as it got upstairs, the brass put me on leave. They said that once whoever's doing all this finds out I've filed a formal complaint, I'd be a sitting duck. They're investigating now, but I don't think they're in much of a hurry—it is a boy's club, after all—so, long story short, I'm available full time for at least a couple of weeks, maybe longer."

Ben nodded, his face a bit less tense.

"Well, then, let me ask—"

"Hush, Ben," said Emily, "we have what we need to know."

She turned to face Constantine. "I like you, I trust you and, if I have to do this, I want you on the job."

Ben nodded.

"Okay," he said. "How will this work?"

"I think we can pretend she's a production assistant. When I'm in the field with Kern, it wouldn't seem too strange if he had somebody helping him—attaching my mic, holding a light, carrying some of the stuff we lug around. She'll look like she's just one of us."

"I like that," said K.B. "It keeps me close and it has an element of surprise, gives me a little edge if somebody approaches, thinking I'm just a hired hand when—"

"When in fact you're her paladin," said Ben. "I concur. But what about the rest of the time, when Kern isn't with you? He wasn't with you when you were in Max's cab, right? What then?"

Emily thought it over.

"When I'm investigating, sniffing around on my own, we'll tell people she's a Northwestern grad student. A Master's candidate in journalism would make sense. She'll be an intern, doing on-the-job training. If anybody objects, she can stand off, but not too far off."

Ben nodded and turned to Constantine.

"It seems clear that you're smart and capable and I don't doubt that you hold your own with your male peers, but, meaning no offense—"

K.B. smiled and nodded.

"I understand, Mr. Winter. Drop that pen."

"What?"

"The pen you're taking notes with," she said. "Drop it."

Ben, puzzled, sat forward in his chair, extended his arm and let the pen drop.

K.B. Constantine moved with speed and purpose, covering the five or six feet between then in an instant. She whipped the baton from her belt and hit the pen squarely, sending it flying.

The pen never hit the floor.

Emily was so stunned that she gasped. Jack Potter smiled.

"No offense taken, Mr. Winter," said K.B. "Rest assured."

Ben pointed at the baton.

"You may put that thing away, ma'am. I have no further questions."

———————

Emily walked out of the planning meeting. K.B. was in a folding chair just outside the door, nursing a cup of coffee and leafing through the *Sun-Times*.

"I've got some desk work to do," said Emily. "You can use the break room until I have to leave."

K.B. shook her head. "I'd rather be in the lobby, keep an eye on the door and folks coming in. You need me, call the front desk."

At her cubicle, Emily scanned literature and a press release Bert had given her, describing something called the Commodore PET, a new device which its manufacturers claimed was a home computer. The device was to be unveiled later that day and Emily had been assigned to interview a computer professor. She set up the interview and started to make some notes about questions she'd ask when her phone rang.

"Winter here."

"Take a close look at Bionni."

"I'm sorry, what? Who is this?"

"The cops dismissed her as a suspect, but they didn't ask the right questions. She shouldn't get away with what she did. Gayle Bionni, you hear? Take a close look."

The line went dead.

Emily sat for just a moment and then dialed the front desk.

"WSMP. How may I direct your call?"

"Janey, it's me, Emily, up in the newsroom. You just sent a call to me."

"Oh, hi. Yes, lady said she would only speak to you."

"Who was it? Did you get a name?"

"No. She asked for you, I put her through. That was it."

"Damn."

K.B. was using her own car, an orange Beetle which had seen its share of Chicago winters and looked it but ran smoothly, the more so because Constantine was a skillful driver. They followed Scott Kern, in the ungainly WSMP station wagon, to the Illinois Institute of Technology where Kern and his "assistant" filmed Emily's interview. The IIT professor speculated that personal computers might eventually have a modest impact on society but that, for most people, the machines were too sophisticated and complicated to be useful in everyday activities. The interview was a struggle—Emily had to constantly interrupt to ask the professor to use language which a TV news audience could understand—but they eventually got enough so that, once edited, it would be suitable for airing.

Kern went back to the studio to edit the piece and then meet Nikki Stone at another assignment. Emily and K.B. headed to Waukegan.

Pet Paradise was noisy and it smelled. The building itself, several small offices in front and two long rows of cages behind, was not in danger of collapsing but it wasn't in great shape, either. There were a dozen dogs in a runway area to one side of the building, barking and growling and sniffing at one another. The odor wafting in the air near the runway was potent.

"Smells worse than it looks," said K.B.

Inside, Emily introduced herself and asked that

the kid behind the counter let Gayle Bionni know she and her intern had arrived. The kid shrugged and pointed.

"You can do that yourself," he said. "Through that door, second door on the left."

Emily knocked on the door.

"Come in."

Gayle Bionni was behind her desk, glasses perched atop her head, a phone at her ear. She was a wiry woman with intense dark eyes and a hawk nose. She waved Emily and K.B. in, pointing at chairs on one side of the room. Emily sniffed the air and looked around until she saw a tall incense stick, a small stream of smoke rising gently from it. The scent was overly sweet but not unwelcome.

"So, Mrs. Phillips, that's the offer. You can spread your donation over the year, so it would be about forty dollars a month at the Boxer level, but you can step up to Retriever or Poodle if you'd care to provide even more support."

Bionni held the phone away from her ear and gestured with her free hand, imitating a chattering mouth with her fingers and mouthing "Blah Blah Blah" silently. Emily thought the gesture, coupled with Bionni's exaggerated eye roll, conveyed contempt for whomever was at the other end of the call.

"No, ma'am," said Bionni, "only the Poodle package includes naming rights to one of our palatial puppy pens. You get a plaque and two tickets to our dinner with the Retriever package. As I said, with the Boxer package, we're offering two seats at the dinner and a bumper sticker."

She held the phone away again, staring at the ceiling. She appeared to be bored and frustrated.

"Mrs. Phillips, let's do this, okay? I'm going to send you our brochure and a simple form you can use to designate your wishes. I'll get that out today and we can talk early next week, okay? Yes, it was nice to talk to you, too. . .no, ma'am, you don't have to decide right away, we just launched this campaign. . .yes, the money will go to the dogs—facilities and kibble and ads in the local publications which help us find a permanent home for the pups. Yes, that is a wonderful service. That's why we want you to be part of it so very much. Yes, ma'am, I'll be in touch. Maybe we can schedule a lunch. Goodbye."

Bionni made a show of sighing loudly and pinching the bridge of her nose.

"Chump change," she said. "I'm scrounging around for chump change these days."

"Hard work," said Emily.

"You have no idea. So, when you called, you said this has something to do with a crime? Unless you're talking about the god-awful smell around here, I don't know how I can help you. And who's this, by the way? You didn't say anything on the phone about two of you."

"This is Karen," said Emily, "she's interning with WSMP, trailing me around and learning how it all works."

"Huh. Well, anyhow, welcome. By the way, Karen, that denim jacket is striking—I quite like it, the embroidery is elegant."

"Thank you," said K.B, and then, with a quick tiny grin, gave Emily a wink.

They had picked out the denim jacket because it was a size too large, just right for concealing the gun and holster nestled against the small of Constantine's back. Emily suppressed a giggle.

"How can I help you?"

"I'm working on the bombing of the Northside Women's Care Clinic," said Emily. "I understand you were employed there."

Bionni's face went sour.

"That place? A snake pit, run by two vipers."

"Dr. Estrada and Ms. Howorth?"

"Bitches. I gave them my best stuff, used my entire Rolodex for them—and it's big, you understand, filled with high dollar prospects—and all they did was show me the door. They didn't know a thing about how fundraising works, but that didn't stop them from pressuring me."

Her tone, exaggerated whining, was plainly unpleasant. She shifted the tone slightly, moving closer to mockery.

"'Where's the money?' 'How much this week?' Pain in the you-know-what, both of them."

"You weren't happy there, then?"

"Didn't like the mission, didn't like the setup. They wouldn't even give me my own office, can you imagine? Had me sit in that big room with everybody else, no privacy. You try making sensitive calls in a room full of chattering women, see how it works for you."

Emily looked at her notepad.

"After they let you go, you told them they would 'pay dearly.' What did you mean by that?"

Bionni snorted.

"So here's the deal, honey. Fundraising's like planting a garden. You pick your plants, you put 'em in the ground, you take care of them, feed them, make sure they're getting enough sun and water. Then you wait. Eventually, you get tomatoes, carrots, peas, maybe blueberries or roses or orchids, but it takes a lot of time and care. The higher the potential donation, the more time it takes. But, they wouldn't wait, they were always impatient. Plus, you know what they put in the budget for meals and travel? A pittance, is what. You can't raise big dollars by taking prospects to lunch at a fast-food joint. Like I say, they didn't have any idea."

"You haven't answered my question," said Emily.

"About them paying? I was talking about the waiting—I would have delivered if they'd given me time. Letting me go let all my prospects go with me. They were going to pay because they wouldn't get the donations I was lining up. That's all."

"Did you think about suing them?"

"I talked to an attorney. He said there wasn't a case. Another idiot."

"So, you were angry with them. You seem angry right now."

"What if I am?"

"Perhaps you wanted to do them harm."

"You aren't serious? You think I bombed that place?"

"Hell hath no fury," said Emily.

"Oh, please. I didn't exactly shed a tear when that place went up—sometimes, you get what you deserve—but I'm hardly the sort of person who blows up buildings."

"Do you live here now?"

"What, Waukegan? Yeah. Had a nifty bachelorette pad, not far from the Loop, but the commute to this place was too long and too expensive, so I gave up my old place and moved. Can't say I like it much, but it's a living, right?"

"You lost your job and a nice apartment, had to move from Chicago to Waukegan—"

Bionni rose from her chair.

"I've had enough, thank you very much. You know the way out—use it. Leave me alone."

"Okay," said Emily. "Just one more question. If you didn't blow up the clinic, who do you think might have done it?"

"Don't know. Don't care. Get out."

"Angry, wasn't she?" said Constantine, firing up the car.

"Yes. I already knew that from the letters she wrote. I suppose it was worth it to confirm that, but I think it was a waste of time. Do you think she could blow up a building?"

"Not a chance," said K.B., "she's unpleasant, no doubt, but violent? And she's got those skinny arms, I'm not sure she could throw a rock hard enough to break a window. I don't think she's got the stuff to light up anything more potent than that yucky jasmine thing."

"I agree," said Emily. "I think somebody sent me on a wild goose chase."

"There are geese in Waukegan? I had no idea."

They both laughed.

"More than an hour up here, it'll take us twice that long, going back in traffic. All a waste of time."

"For you, maybe," said Constantine.

"And for you."

"True, but I'm not the one trying to find a bomber."

"What's that mean?"

"Let's say I'm the bomber. If I know you're trying to find me and I suspect you're getting closer, what would I do?"

Emily looked over at K.B. and studied her face for a moment.

"You'd distract me. You'd send me off in another direction. You'd arrange for me to waste my time."

"You bet I would," said Constantine. "I might even take a shot at you."

"I wonder who made that call," said Emily.

Chapter Fourteen

"I'm headed to the bar," said Lois Lipton. "Anybody need anything?"

"I'll have another glass of wine," said Linda Marshall, "and see if you can snag a bowl of pretzels, too."

"Don't bother," said Mary Massey, "they're stale."

"That's always confused me," said Emily. "How do we know when a pretzel is stale? Aren't they stale coming out of the bag?"

"I don't care," said Marshall, "I'm hungry."

"How about you, K.B.," said Lipton, "you need another beer?"

"I'm good."

"You've been here close to an hour," said Becca Bloomfield, "and that bottle's still nearly full. You're not doing your part. You want to run with the big girls, you got to keep up."

K.B. laughed.

"Emily told me it might be a long night," she said, "I'm just pacing myself."

"So, Emily," said Kirsten Bonner, "did you follow up with that guy, wanted to sell us his buildings?"

"I did, and thanks again for the tip," said Emily. "It came up empty. He's in financial limbo—can't collect on the insurance until the investigation closes, can't unload a pile of burned rubble without taking a serious loss. If he torched the building, he did himself far more harm than good and, near as I can tell, he's too greedy to do that."

"Anything else look promising?"

"No. The RTLC people won't talk, their angel, guy named Jon Haskill, was outright angry when I tried to question him."

Lois Lipton returned with two drinks and a half-empty bowl of pretzels. Marshall grabbed a handful.

"You guys talking about NWCC? I talked to one of the cops working that case today, just to get caught up. They're stumped. You got something, Emily? You going to scoop me?"

"Nope. I was just telling everybody I'm not getting anywhere."

"Frustrating, this one," said Lipton, "let's change the subject. Mary, that guy at the end of the bar, blazer and striped shirt, isn't that your new anchor?"

Massey glanced at the bar.

"Mark Parsons. That's him."

"Looks good to me," said Lipton. "You know his story? Married, dating, what?"

Massey smiled.

"Don't bother," she said. "He came in from D.C. We thought he'd add some weight to our anchor desk, but I don't think he's going to last."

"Why not?" asked Emily.

"He doesn't really get the city, thinks local politics aren't important enough, keeps talking about missing the battles in Congress. Plus, he insists on writing his own copy and he writes like he's with a newspaper—way too long and deep. I had to guess, I'd say he'll walk on us, first offer he gets. The only question is whether he pulls the trigger or we do. Either way, he's not going to be around long."

"Another empty promise," said Lipton, "and he's so good looking. I'm telling you, girls, there aren't any good men anywhere."

Bloomfield and Bonner raised their glasses.

"Amen."

"Hear, hear."

They kept at it for another hour before Ben walked into the room and approached the table.

"Good evening, ladies. Charmed to see you all, as ever."

He gave them a little bow and nodded at Constantine.

"Hi, K.B. All is well with you, I trust. Anything to report?"

She glanced at Emily and gave Ben a knowing stare.

"Have I offended? I hope not."

Emily stood and joined him. She leaned in to give him a kiss and then whispered to him.

"They don't know," she said.

Ben blushed.

Lipton saw the exchange and grinned.

"Why, Ms. Winter, I believe you've just made an indecent proposition. In public, no less. Have you no shame?"

Emily smiled.

"Actually, I told him he's paying for dinner this evening and that embarrassed him. Ben's on top of most things, but he tends to forget that he's out of cash. Which he almost always is. Am I right, darling? Did you also leave your wallet on the dresser?"

Ben offered a sheepish grin.

"Guilty as charged," he said.

"Such a surprise. No matter, dinner's on me," she said. "You all have a great evening and a fun weekend. K.B., I'll see you bright and early Monday. Take care, friends."

On the sidewalk, Ben said, "You haven't told them somebody took a shot at you?"

"I haven't," she said. "It would only distress them. K.B. wouldn't leave me until you showed up, so she came along. Since we all get together to unwind and talking about that shot just makes me tense and nervous, I just put it aside."

"You can do that? Just ignore it?"

"Not really, but at least I got to leave it behind for an hour or so."

"I admire your determination," said Ben. "I can't think about anything else. I was not precisely thrilled to see Ms. Constantine joining in the libations."

"She wasn't," said Emily. "She ordered a beer and took exactly two sips. I counted. Then she just moved it around on the table so it looked like she was drinking. She was on the job as usual."

"Well, there's that," he said.

Bert Presley took a sip of coffee. His tone and mood were serious.

"It stands to reason, doesn't it? You're getting too close to somebody and they wanted to warn you off, scare you off?"

"I can't think of another explanation, Bert," said Emily, "but if we're right it still doesn't get us anywhere. I've gotten nothing but silence from the RTLC crowd. Randy Hoffman just doesn't make sense as a suspect. If he bombed his own building, he shot himself in the foot when he did it."

"I think that's a mixed metaphor. Or maybe a bad pun. Wasn't there a kid you were looking at?"

"Terhune. As far as I know, he's in Connecticut. I never thought him a likely choice—he's too, what, too mild? Maybe too thoughtful. Plus, he's well removed from RTLC's leadership and I didn't sense he had a commitment to them. He had his own agenda."

"You've explored other possible leads, right?"
Emily nodded.

"I went through their hate mail file. It didn't produce anything except the angry ex-employee, Gail Bionni. I don't think she bombed the building and neither does K.B. Constantine. I do wonder who tipped me to Bionni, but, tip or not, I don't believe she's the bomber."

"You said she got angry with you. Angry enough to—"

"'Angry' is too strong, Bert. She was peeved, but I think that has more to do with her new job than me. You want to go down that path, Jon Haskill was angrier than Bionni, but I didn't get a thing from him. He shut me down cold, before I could even ask any questions. I don't think he sees me as a threat. His stonewall is as solid as all the others and, since he won't talk to me, he doesn't even know what I know."

"Which is nothing."

"Exactly."

"Okay, you got dead ends. Normally, I'd just let it slide but I don't think we can do that."

"I sure can't. The story's too important."

"That, too," said Presley, "but what I had in mind was we need to stay on this until we find out who took a shot at you. So long as this thing drags on, somebody out there will continue to think you're a threat. If you're a threat, then you're a target. That's not acceptable, period."

"Trust me, I get that. But I'm not sure what to do at this point."

"When did you last talk to Potter? Maybe his crew has turned something up."

"I don't think so," said Emily. "My pal Lipton, at the *Trib*, touched base with somebody on Potter's team last Friday and she says they're not getting anywhere either."

"Check with him anyhow. Maybe the two of you will think of something new."

"Okay."

"One more thing, Winter."

"What?"

"Your bodyguard, K.B."

"What about her?"

"You and Ben paying for that?"

"Yes, we are."

"I talked with Malafronte. He and I agree that we, the station, I mean, we're responsible. You're working on a story for us, that story puts you in jeopardy, we're responsible."

"I don't—"

"Simple. Tell Ben to send her bills to us. You work for us, we pay for your protection."

"You're kidding. Didn't you just tell me, couple weeks ago, the news budget is in rough shape."

"Doesn't matter, Emily. We're covering the costs."

"Bert, I don't know what to say."

He leaned back and put his feet on his desk.

"Think of it this way. You're a valuable piece of the puzzle around here. You're not up there in Billy Hutchins territory, but you're close. What we're doing is protecting ourselves. Enlightened self-interest, see?"

"Now you're going to make me blush."

"Not in my office, lady. Don't even think about it. Besides, I don't have time for it—I got work to do and, need I point out, so do you."

———————

The cage was large. The tiger pacing around in it was sizable, too.

Jack Potter was sitting on a bench, working on a tuna fish sandwich and watching the animal pace. Emily watched him watching for a moment before she approached and sat on the bench beside him.

"Hey, Nails. Hi."

He shifted his gaze to her as she opened her satchel and extracted a sandwich of her own.

"Whatcha got?"

"Ben's meatloaf. Had it for dinner over the weekend, it was terrific, but it's even better cold."

"Looks good," said Potter. "I got half a tuna here, you want to swap half of yours for it?"

Emily laughed.

"No, sir. No chance."

"Damn. So, what's up?"

"Same old," said Emily, "just checking in on the NWCC investigation."

"Nothing to check. We've verified Carol Lobes' alibi—she told us she was home getting everybody ready for school and work. One of her neighbors saw her on the sidewalk in front of her house, around 7:00 a.m., picking up the morning paper. It's close to an hour, driving from her place to NWCC, in good traffic. By 6:30 a.m., quarter to 7:00 a.m., she'd hit early rush hour. She might have been able to get there at 6:00 a.m., but there's no way she could get there, fire bomb the place, and be back in her front yard by 7:00 a.m."

"I don't suppose she had access to a helicopter?" Potter chuckled.

"Nope. And I think folks on Clark Street would have noticed a bird landing in front of the clinic."

"What about Norman Brent, then? What's his alibi?"

"Home in bed. He lives alone, so there's no verification, but one of his neighbors saw him wheeling garbage cans out to the street around 9:30 a.m., maybe 10:00 a.m."

"He's much closer, right? Just across the Evanston line in Skokie."

"Yeah. He might have hustled down to Clark and back again, but he'd have traffic issues too. More to the point, we haven't got anything else to lead us in his direction. No evidence, nobody saw him near the clinic—except when he was on the picket line, of course—and he flatly denies he did it. Nothing to work with there."

They nibbled at their food and watched the tiger pace.

"I went through the hate mail Carmen Howorth has," said Emily. "She says you did, too. I found one lead but it didn't pan out. You?"

"Same. We borrowed the file and copied it so we could split them up and work them over. Somebody else found the Bionni letters, but we didn't even think she was worth a visit. You get anything from her?"

"A lot of spite and some anger, but nothing else. Same thing with the kid, Terhune, I interviewed while he was picketing. He's got some anger and he did act on it, but not at the level of arson and murder."

"Act on it how?"

"Do you have to know? It was minor vandalism, he's left for college and, bottom line, he's a good kid. If I tell you what he did and you guys go after him, it'll only screw up his life. I don't think he needs that and, more to the point, I don't believe for a minute that he blew the place up."

"I'll let it slide, then. But if I have to lean on you at some point, you're going to have to tell me. You know that, right?"

Potter gave her his *I mean it* stare. Emily nodded emphatically.

"Got it," she said.

"One more thing," said Potter. "I've put the word out about the shooting, got a bunch of guys keeping their eyes and ears open, but I haven't heard anything. K.B. still keeping an eye on you?"

"She is. She drove me over here. I suspect she's somewhere near us right now, waiting until we're done. She told me to tell you she figures I'm almost as safe in your company as I am in hers."

"Almost?"

"Her words, Jack. Verbatim."

He smiled.

"She's probably right. She's got about ten years on me and she's in better shape, too."

Potter raised his plastic drinking glass and took a long sip of lemonade. Emily watched the tiger again.

"He reminds me of us," said Emily.

"The cat? How so?"

"Prowling around with no place to go, can't stop moving but isn't moving toward anything. He's on the prowl because it's what he does, even if there's no prey in sight."

"And, in his case, there never will be."

"And there's the difference," said Emily. "He's in a cage, we're not. He can't go find his prey, but we're free to go wherever we need to."

"Wherever that is," said Potter. "I hate cases like this. Everybody thinks it's so exciting, working homicide, catching bad guys. Nobody thinks about the ones we don't close. The longer it takes, the less likely we are to succeed. This one feels like that to me—we may not be caged, but we aren't getting anywhere."

"We haven't gotten anywhere yet, Jack. But we haven't quit, either. Truth is, I can't quit."

"Yeah," he said, "me either."

He opened his sandwich and scraped the remaining tuna onto one half off the bread. He balled the empty half-slice, stood and tossed it into the cage. The tiger leapt on it and devoured it. He stared at Potter for a moment, waiting to see if more food was in the offing. When none came, the animal returned to prowling.

Emily was walking across the WSMP parking lot after lunch, K.B. at her side, when she stopped dead in her tracks.

Constantine looked concerned. "You okay?"

"I think so," said Emily. "I just had a troubling thought."

"What?"

"Did you tell Potter we drove up to Waukegan last week?"

"Nope. I haven't seen Jack, except to wave when you guys finished lunch today, since I started shadowing you. Why do you ask?"

"Because I don't have the faintest idea how he knew I'd interviewed Gayle Bionni."

Chapter Fifteen

Carmen Howorth stood at the portable podium set up in one corner of a vacant lot. Several members of the NWCC board and staff stood in a semi-circle behind her. There was a uniformed Chicago police officer at each end of the arc, their side arms and batons prominently on display. The officer on the left side was glowering at the thirty or so people gathered in front of the podium; he was more than a little heavy, his shirt partially untucked where his considerable belly tugged at it. He was standing next to Alicia Good, smartly dressed in a tailored tan suit with a crisp Oxford blue blouse. Emily found the contrast amusing.

Given recent history, a public assemblage of NWCC staff and supporters generated a police presence. In addition to the two facing the group, there were three other uniformed officers scattered through the crowd and, Emily suspected, an under-cover cop or two on hand as well. The event, in Chicago just south of the Evanston border, had been posted on the City Newswire morning budget and

NWCC had invited patients and donors, too, so the gathering wasn't a secret. Since there had been no arrests for the bombing, the cops assumed NWCC was still a target and they weren't taking any chances.

"Good morning," said Carmen Howorth. "Thank you for joining us today. On behalf of the NWCC community, I am proud to announce that we will begin construction next week on a brand new clinic at this location.

"I want to thank our board of directors for their tireless efforts to secure the funds necessary to undertake this project. They have given NWCC new life by relentlessly soliciting donations. I see two or three donors who have been especially generous among you—we are blessed to have your support—and I also want to specifically express our gratitude to Mid-Point Savings and Loan for working with us to create a financing package which gives us the flexibility to pay for the construction and move into our new home as quickly as possible.

"Finally, I am both saddened and honored to announce that the new Northwest Women's Choice Clinic building will be named for our founder and our heroine, Joan Estrada. The building which rises here will be known as 'Dr. J's House.'"

A smattering of applause broke out as Howorth and several members of the board gently wiped tears from their cheeks.

When the applause began, Emily instinctively raised her hands to join in. She froze for a second, shook her head emphatically, and dropped her hands to her side. Scott Kern, standing beside her, his camera on a tripod, pointed at the podium, watched her with a quizzical look.

WBBM's reporter on the scene held up her hand and Howorth nodded at her.

"Ms. Howorth, how have you managed your patient's care since your clinic was destroyed? Are women still getting the services they want?"

"I won't disclose any specifics," said Howorth, "but we are in constant touch with our patients, working with them to coordinate services with other facilities. Our nurses are working at several locations so they are able to continue working with some of our patients. We have interviewed several highly impressive women, but we have not yet selected a new Medical Director. We aren't as efficient or as accessible as we were before the bombing, but we're doing the best we can. Getting this new facility up and running is a top priority for us."

A reporter from the NBC affiliate took a step forward.

"Miss Howorth, can you tell us anything about the investigation into that bombing? Do you believe the police are any closer to finding out who destroyed the Clark street clinic?"

Howorth winced.

"I have no information," she said. "Like every-one else, we continue to hope that the person who attacked us will be brought to justice, but beyond that, I have nothing to add. I will point out that Connie Beck, who is a deputy in the Police Department's communications office, is here today and I believe she can answer your questions about the investigation once our dedication is completed. And it is time to do just that."

Howorth and the board members moved forward. Several of them picked up shovels and they all bent over and, in unison, turned a little bit of earth. The TV crews, including Scott Kern, filmed the action as still photographers took a battery of shots; the audience applauded and a few cheered.

The gathering then moved to a temporary table laid out with coffee urns, sweet rolls and paper plates. They milled about, chatting and smiling. Howorth and her board moved through the group, approaching donors and expressing their appreciation; Emily concluded that they had divided a list of key donors to be personally thanked.

Emily flipped her notepad shut and walked over to Scott Kern; he was packing up his gear.

"You get everything you needed?"

"Of course. The statement, start to finish, the Q and A and that stupid shovel thing. You'd think somebody would come up with a better shot for us—everybody's been doing the shovel bit for years. It's boring, you know?"

Emily smiled.

"It is. It's cut above holding up an oversized check, but it's still pretty trite. On the other hand, you know Bert's going to use it tonight and, after all, that's why they do it. They're in the fundraising business. The exposure might lure some money for the cause."

"I'd pay 'em to dream up a better shot," said Kern.

"How much?"

He chuckled.

"Not enough to make the shovels go away. I can't afford it."

"Then I guess we'll just have to live with it," said Emily. "Let's do the stand-up."

With the group behind her, Emily looked into Kern's camera and spoke.

"The Northside Women's Choice Center broke ground today for a new facility here on the north side of Chicago. The organization's former clinic, on Clark Street, was destroyed by arson, but today NWCC's staff and board launched a new phase of their work to ensure healthcare and family planning services for the women of Chicago. Soliciting additional funding for this new facility, NWCC's leadership rejoiced as their new home rises, almost literally, from the ashes."

Emily dropped her mic to her side, frowning.

"Scott, can you play it back for me, please."

He handed her his headset. She listened and her frown grew deeper.

"I might as well have asked people to send a check," she said. "And that nonsense about rising from the ashes isn't reporting, it's joining the party."

"If you say so," said Scott.

"I do. That last sentence has to go, Scott. If I forget, remind me. I won't let that go on air."

"Okay," he said and then, with a sly grin, "good thing I didn't shoot your standing ovation, isn't it?"

"You saw that? Forgot who I am for a moment. Next time we cover this story, remind me that I'm not on the staff at NWCC—I can't seem to remember that on my own these days."

"You got it."

As they made their way to WSMP's ungainly station wagon, Connie Beck broke away from the crowd and headed toward Emily. Emily thought Beck was going to offer an interview and slowed her pace, but Beck walked right past her. As she passed, Beck spoke in a voice just above a whisper.

"Have fun in Waukegan, Winter?"

Emily stared at her. Beck's stern demeanor broke for just a second, long enough to expose a mean little grin, and then she strode on and approached the NBC reporter.

Kern watched her walk away.

"What the hell was that?"

Emily paused, pondering, and then said, "I believe that was the voice of the woman who gave me what was supposed to be a hot tip last week."

K.B. Constantine joined them.

"You think Beck tipped you to Bionni?"

"You bet I do," said Emily.

"Why would she do that?"

"Another volley in a grudge match."

K.B. looked perplexed.

"I got it," said Kern. "Gary Easton, right?"

"Bet the ranch on it," said Emily. "He made it clear that I wasn't going to get anything from the department on the bombing. If it weren't for Potter, I wouldn't have a clue about what's going on in that investigation."

"I still don't get it," said K.B.

"The illustrious Mr. Easton is convinced I'm the devil incarnate," said Emily. "I guess he wasn't satisfied just locking me out of the story, so he had his flunky send me off on a wild goose chase."

"Wow. That's pretty low."

Kern snorted.

"You're too kind," he said. "That S.O.B. starts at low and goes down from there. Stunts like that aren't beneath him because nothing is beneath him. He's an ass."

"I won't argue with you," said Emily.

K.B. climbed into the back seat of the wagon.

"You going to pay him back?"

"I certainly hope so," said Emily with a crooked smile, "but I'm going to have to think about it first."

"One of the nice things about daylight saving time," said Ben, "is the opportunity to indulge in an evening stroll."

They were in their small kitchen. Ben was

washing dishes, Emily drying and storing them away.

"I presume that is an invitation."

"Your perception is as keen as ever," said Ben. "I thought we might wander down to the marina and gaze at the boats."

They left their building and headed north, walking along the edge of Lincoln Park and under the bridge which served as the Lake Shore Drive exit ramp to Belmont. Belmont Harbor was awash in water craft, older junkers beside sleek new sail boats, small craft snuggled into berths adjacent to cabin cruisers large enough to be summer homes. They made their way to the spit of land which bordered the entrance from the lake to the harbor. Ben strolled slowly, gazing at the boats; Emily faced Lake Michigan, watching it grow darker as the sun fell behind the tall apartment and condo buildings along Sheridan Road.

"One wonders, living so close to this treasure," said Ben, "if one ought not consider the purchase of a craft of one's own."

Emily turned and paused a beat before she laughed.

"Let me count the ways, dear. We can't afford a boat. Even if we could, the cost of lifting it out of the harbor to store it for the winter would explode our budget. Then, there's this: I don't particularly relish the idea of being tossed about in something which one good gust of Chicago wind might capsize. And, much as I love you, and Lord knows I do, I don't think either one of us could maintain a boat."

"All true," said Ben, "and yet—"

"I remember when, several months ago, you were convinced that we had to have a cat."

"You raise that with cause, I trust."

"Do you recall why we decided it wasn't a great idea?"

"I believe we concluded that our erratic work schedules would have made a feline in the family feel neglected."

"I think we actually concluded that we'd probably end up starving the poor creature."

Ben laughed.

"Too right."

"Don't you think the same principle applies here? If we owned a boat—"

"We'd end up sinking it?"

"Maybe. More likely we'd end up spending an hour or two driving it around and the rest of the time fretting about it. And paying for it."

"I believe the proper term is 'sailing,' not 'driving,' but your point is well taken."

"Sorry to dash your dreams, pal."

"Oh, you haven't dashed the dream at all, m'love. The dream is still very much alive, even as it is pure whimsy. That one, for example, is so handsome that I can easily imagine standing on its bow at sunset."

"Imagination is a good thing," said Emily. "Being broke is not."

Dusk faded quickly and the lake grew dark. Emily turned for one more look and the vast expanse of water seemed to change before her eyes, a certain aura of calm and serenity giving way to something more foreboding. She imagined being out on the water in the dark, unable to determine in which direction lay land or, more ominously, deeper darker water. She shivered. Ben saw it and moved to her side, wrapping an arm around her.

"Let's go home," he said.

"Yes, please."

They were walking back across the park in front of their building when Emily heard a noise—a fire cracker? she wondered—and Ben fell to the ground. He rolled on his side and lunged for his thigh. Emily saw the blood on his trousers and screamed.

She went to her knees—an involuntary movement because she felt too weak to stand—and leaned in. Ben was staring at his leg, one hand pressed hard against it.

"I believe I've been shot," he said. "It hurts."

Emily wasn't sure what to do. Her first instinct was to race to the street and flag down a car. She remembered that St. Joseph's Hospital was only a block or so down the Inner Drive, so help was nearby. But she couldn't decide whether to run there for help—she didn't want to leave him—or help him up and support him so they could walk there.

She looked up to see if any cars or people were nearby. It had grown dark enough that cars were using headlights. As she stood, unsteadily, to move, she saw a figure racing out of the park and across the street; the runner dashed in front of a car and was, for just a moment, illuminated in its lights. The figure disappeared and the car kept going.

"I believe I can walk," said Ben. "St. Joe's is close enough, I can make it if you let me lean on you."

He stood, haltingly, and began moving, dragging his injured leg behind him.

"No," said Emily. "I don't think it's safe for you to try. Wait here. I'm going to flag down a car."

She trotted toward the Inner Drive and arrived at the sidewalk just as a car came up Wellington toward her. She stepped into the street and waved both arms at the driver. The driver honked at her but slowed and then stopped. Emily ran to the driver's side of the car.

"My husband's been injured," she said. "Could you please help me get him into your car and drive him to the Emergency Room? He's losing blood."

The driver, a middle-aged woman, stared at Emily, hesitating.

"Please. He's been shot."

The woman stuck an arm out and pointed behind Emily.

"Is that your husband?"

Emily turned and looked. Benjamin had managed to reach the curb.

"Yes. If you just pull over by the sidewalk, I'll get him into the back seat."

The woman hesitated.

"Is this for real? You're not planning to rob me or something, are you?"

Emily fought down his instinct to scream at the woman.

"I'm Emily Winter, WSMP News. We live just there"—she pointed to their condo—"and we need your help."

The woman squinted at her.

"I know you!"

The car edged to the curb and Emily pulled a back door open. Ben, grimacing and moving awkwardly, was sweating and his face was pale. He flopped onto the seat and Emily climbed in next to the woman.

"Right down there," she said, pointing. "There's a driveway. You can pull up to the Emergency Room entrance."

Emily left Ben in the back seat and ran into the ER. She spotted a nurse and shouted.

"My husband is wounded. He's in the back seat out there. I need help. Please hurry, he's bleeding and I think he's going to pass out."

The nurse hollered at two men sitting behind the ER desk and they sprang, wheeling a cart through the doors. With their help, Ben climbed onto the gurney and they raced back toward the entrance. Emily ran beside them, but when they reached the door she stopped and turned toward the car. The woman slid over to lean across the front seat and reach the back door. She pulled it shut, scooted back behind the wheel, waved at Emily and drove away.

"He's going to be fine," said the attending ER physician. "We cleaned the wound and stitched it up. Small caliber gun, the wound isn't very big, the bullet didn't hit a bone or any tendons. 'Through and through' is what the cops say. If we were in a cowboy movie, I could say 'It's only a flesh wound.'

"You should bring him back tomorrow when we've got a full staff or check in with your own doctor to make sure everything is secure and healing. I've given him a dose of antibiotics, just to be safe, and the nurse will give you a prescription—he's got enough meds in him now to get him through the night, but tomorrow, fill the order and get him started on it. Twice a day for ten days to prevent an infection. Got that?

"Yes," said Emily. She was standing by the gurney, one hand on Ben's shoulder and the other holding his hand. Ben was conscious but looked hazy; his face was drawn and sallow.

"There's one more thing," said the doctor. "We're required to file a police report. As far as I know, it never makes any difference. I mean, they take evidence from us, like the bullets and all, but we never hear from them again and I don't think they usually catch anybody. But, still, we'll file the report. You probably should, too."

"I've got direct connections. Several, in fact. I'll make sure they know all about this."

"Good. It's going to take a while for those stitches to do their job. I'd say ten days, maybe two weeks. He can walk, although he'll probably be uncomfortable for the next couple of days. It might be a good idea to get him a cane so he can support himself and ease the pressure on that leg while it heals."

Ben stirred and gave Emily's hand a squeeze. She leaned over, kissed him on the forehead and bent her head so she could hear his drug-muted voice.

"Capital," said Ben. "I've always admired gentlemen who move about with a stylish walking stick. Now I can join their fraternity without appearing to be a fop."

Emily smiled, kissed him again and then—to her amazement—burst into tears which she could neither control nor stop. As she wept, Ben squeezed her hand again.

Chapter Sixteen

"I should have been there." K.B. Constantine was standing at the living room windows, staring across the street to the spot where Ben had been shot. "I would have caught him."

"He was gone before I could even think," said Emily. "I think you're right, it was a man, but he was running and he had a big head start."

"Tall? White? Heavy or thin? Blond? Beard?"

"I don't know. Tallish, maybe, but he was already in the street before I saw him, so I'm not sure. I think he had on a tee shirt. I think it was blue. Sneakers—you know, gym shoes. Jeans, I think, but it's all blurry. I was trying to get help, I wasn't really focused on him."

"Did it say anything?"

"I don't understand—"

"The tee shirt. A Bears shirt? Cubs? Any lettering? Maybe a slogan or something cute."

"Maybe lettering. It wasn't plain, there was something on it but I didn't see it well enough or, if I did, I can't remember. I should have been sharper."

"Nonsense," said K.B., "you were in shock. Most victims have trouble remembering stuff about a perp who stood face to face with them. You got help and took care of Ben, that's what's important."

Emily had taken the day off. Ben was prone on the couch, dozing and still somewhat hazy from his pain medication.

"K.B.," he said, "are you free to stay and keep an eye on Emily? I know we agreed that your services would not be required when I am in her company, but I'm not sure I'd be any more helpful to her today than I was yester evening."

"I'll stay," she said, "but you don't need to beat yourself up about this. It was dark, right? The guy was behind a tree, maybe using it to steady his shot? You didn't see him because you couldn't see him. If I'd been there, I would probably have missed him, too. You're not responsible for this. The shooter is."

"Still," said Ben. He attempted to sit up. "Oopsy-daisy, not quite ready for that yet."

He eased back, adjusted a pillow and closed his eyes.

Emily and K.B. moved to the dining area and sat at the table.

"I'm trying to remember what I saw," said Emily, "but it's not working. You know that feeling, when you forget something but it isn't gone, it's just out of reach?"

"Sure," said K.B., "Last night, I was standing in front of the fridge, the door open, but I couldn't think why I was there."

"Exactly," said Emily. "I'm sure that I saw something, but I'm certain I don't know what. Frustrating."

"Let it go," said K.B. 'It'll be there eventually."

"I hope so. So, I need to make a few phone calls. You be okay sitting around?"

K.B. rose and walked to the entry hall, returning with copies of the *Sun-Times* and the *Tribune*.

"Two sports sections," she said. "I'll read 'em both. Hardly ever get to even one, so this is cool. I'm happy."

"Good."

Emily called Carmen Howorth. She didn't answer. Emily pulled a small address book from her satchel and flipped through it, finding and dialing Alicia Good's office.

"This is Alicia."

"Hi, pal. It's Emily."

"Hello. Sorry I didn't have time to chat yesterday. I had to deal with three of the donors who were there. One of them wouldn't stop talking and by the time she finally did, you were gone. Good report last night—thanks for that. I was hoping you'd be on the air."

"Scott and I edited it when we got back to the studio and Bert decided to let the anchors do the intro, so they didn't need me. That's not why I called, though."

Emily told her friend about the evening's tribulations.

"Lord, I had no idea," said Alicia. "Is he okay? That's horrible."

"He's fine. Well, he's kind of loaded right now, but the doctor says he'll be like new in no time."

"That's good news," said Alicia.

"It sure is. So, here's why I called. Did you happen to notice anybody out of place at the event? A stranger, probably a guy."

Alicia paused, considering.

"I don't think so," she said. "I recognized the donors we'd invited, of course, especially the ones I was told to thank in person. Almost all our staff were there. The others were patients, I think, and a handful of Joan's friends. And the others on the board, of course. But strangers? None. Well, I don't know the cops who were there, but I guess they're not what you mean."

"Right you are. Gary Easton might enjoy taking a shot at me, but I don't think he's that brave. It was a long shot to begin with, there's no reason to assume that the shooter was also at the event, but I thought I'd ask."

"You free for lunch? We could go somewhere with a patio, you could relax, maybe have a glass of wine."

"So sweet," said Emily, "but I think I want to stick around here, keep an eye on Ben."

"Of course. Who's keeping an eye on you? You and Ben hired somebody, right?"

"K.B. She's sitting right here," said Emily.

"She's the bodyguard, right? I haven't told anybody about her, like you asked—well, Greg of course, but nobody else. Give Ben a hug for me, okay?"

"Happily," said Emily.

"And if you guys need anything, Greg and I are officially on call from this moment forward."

"Thanks," said Emily. "You're the best."

She turned her chair and looked out the windows facing the park and the lake beyond. She estimated where she and Ben had been when she heard the shot and then tried to guess where the shooter had been. She considered the direction they had taken on their way home and matched that with the trajectory of the bullet when it hit Ben's leg. She envisioned the route the shooter—if the running figure she'd seen was in fact the shooter—had taken. She was almost sure she had it all right, but she was equally sure that it didn't make much difference. She closed her eyes for a moment and pictured the figure cutting across the street but the image she conjured up was still indistinct. She sighed and turned away from the windows.

She rose and walked over to the couch, confirming that Ben was asleep. She wandered down the hall toward their bedroom, paced around it for a little while, then wandered back again. Ben was asleep and K.B. was still deep in the Sports pages. When Emily padded back to the dining table, K.B. looked up.

"You look tired," she said. "I'm here all day, so if you'd like to take a nap—"

"I admit last night took a lot out of me, but I'd

rather slog through it and sleep well tonight. When I was working the early morning shift—up at 3:30 a.m.—I tried napping but it just made getting up that early even harder."

"You're a pretty tough cookie, huh?"

Emily shook her head.

"I just do what I have to," she said. "Besides, I'm a bit too petite to be tough, don't you think?"

"You're kidding, right?"

"Not at all. Why?"

"Well, think about it, girl. You worked impossible hours all week and the way I picture it, there were a bunch of guys making your work harder every single day. Jack Potter told me you just about single-handedly brought down Tommy Jameson and he says you solved the CARD murder when all the homicide guys thought it was a dead case."

"That's my job," said Emily. "It's what I do. Lots of women are out there doing the same kind of thing, pushing through the barriers and doing good work. Look at you, for instance. You didn't just qualify for the force, you had to over-qualify 'cause the guys were convinced you couldn't do it."

"I won't argue that," said K.B., "but there's something else."

"What?"

"Emily, somebody's tried to kill you. Twice. Most of the cops I know haven't come close to pressure like that—some of 'em on the force for decades, never once draw a pistol. Two shots, right? And the first thing you did, once you were sure Ben'd be okay, you get on the phone and investigate. Tough as nails, you ask me."

"Potter tell you that?"

"He told me why he calls you Nails, yes, but my view is my own. Heck, Emily, you don't even look like you're scared."

Emily laughed.

"Between us girls," she said, "I'm scared all the time. When I was at the radio station, I walked in every morning terrified that I'd make a mistake—a big one—and I'd never work in news again."

"Not the same as being shot at."

"Okay, good point. But that's just a weird kind of incentive."

"How so?"

"It seems pretty clear that somebody is trying to scare me off the job, right? Why else? I'm working on the NWCC bombing, somebody doesn't want me to find out who the bomber is. When I get that kind of resistance—you know, the radio guys treating me like a cute token, Gary Easton, when he was at WSMP, trying to sabotage everything I did—it just makes me try that much harder."

"Tough," said K.B.

"Maybe determined. Persistent, I guess. I'll tell you this, though—I was as scared as I've ever been last night. Before I saw where Ben had been hit, the only thing I could think of was that I was going to lose him. That's the most terrifying thing I can imagine."

"Well, you didn't lose him."

"True. But, you do see, don't you, that now I'm past that, I have even more reason to do my job."

"You want to catch the guy who shot your husband."

"Right this minute," said Emily. "I'm fanatical about it."

"Too fanatical to have some lunch?"

Emily grinned.

"Nope."

"Good, 'cause I'm starving."

K.B. left the condominium and walked briskly from Wellington to Diversey. There was a walk-up falafel stand near the corner and the guy behind the counter had the order Emily had phoned in waiting—meatball sandwiches, a generous side of falafel and a green salad. The clerk gave her a paper sack with string handles and she toted it back.

When she came into the condo, Emily was smiling.

"I've got it," she said.

"You know who shot at you?"

"Not that. Still can't dredge it up, don't have a clue."

"What, then?"

"I figured out how to pay Gary Easton back."

Emily, Ben and K.B. sat at the table; the two women nibbled while Ben devoured his sandwich, most of the falafel and at least half of the salad.

Ben was up and showered before Emily stirred from her sleep the next morning.

"Good morning," she said. "You're up early."

"And ready to go to work," said Ben.

"You're sure? You don't want to take one more day?"

"Certainly not," he said. "Besides, if I get off the bus a stop or two early, I can walk through the Loop with my cane. The odds are excellent that I'll be the only fellow afoot with a walking stick. How splendid is that?"

"Super splendid," said Emily. "Gimme a kiss."

He did.

Chapter Seventeen

"Happy Friday, folks. And a Friday in the dead of summer, at that," said Bert Presley. "City Hall's quiet, nobody got shot up last night, D.C. is on its summer break, schools are closed, half the city is out of town and I'm betting the other half are on their way."

"Lots of weather, then?" said Emily.

"Yeah. Things get slow, we turn Billy loose for an extra minute, maybe ninety seconds. He loves that and we know everybody in ChicagoLand loves our Billy, so it's a double win. We'll probably expand the sports block, too."

One of the producers raised a hand.

"Mark?"

"So, we all get the day off?"

"Not while I'm in this chair. You read the morning papers, you'll know that New York City went dark for hours yesterday and last night—total blackout. We've got some footage from a local station back there, shows the whole city from the air, dark as a dungeon. That's a good hook. Suggestions?"

Emily said, "I've got a contact at Com Ed, I could

check in and see if we can get one of their people to tell us how they're prepared for a blackout here, maybe provide some tips, what to do when the power goes out."

"Not bad," said Presley. "Anybody else?"

Nikki Stone leaned forward. "I know a guy in a brokerage firm. I could get him to explain how they tried to keep doing business without access to Wall Street."

"I like that."

Don Malafronte said, "I wonder what happens to wire transfers, electronic payments when this happens. Wouldn't that mess up business deals?"

"It might," said Presley. "Mark, make a couple calls, see where that leads. While you're at it, I think I saw a story said that some college in the city has its own generator, so they were the only place in town with power. Let's find out if that's an option here—maybe hospitals, cop precincts, fire stations? We get enough, we'll lead with it all."

"'Team 8 will help you through dark times,'" said Malafronte. "We can promo it in the day parts."

"Oh, sure, that'll work," said Emily, "all we have to do is ignore the fact that if the power's out, so are we."

"Always good to hear from you, Winter," said Presley. "Let's get to work."

———————

The woman who called the police department's

headquarters after lunch that Friday refused to leave a message. She said she would talk with Gary Easton, nobody else. Miranda, the secretary in the communications office, used the intercom to tell Easton about the call.

"She says she's got a hot tip, boss. Won't share it with anybody but you."

"She say why?"

Miranda giggled.

"She says she used to tune in WSMP news every day when you worked there. She watched their noon news and early evening and then the ten o'clock broadcast and she says she did it just to see you. She says she really admires you and she knows she can trust you."

"Okay," said Easton. "Put her through."

The caller told him that she was a friend of Gayle Bionni. Earlier in the day, when they'd been chatting, Bionni told her that a reporter working on that 'bombing thing' had interviewed Bionni. Easton smiled and told her he was aware of that.

"I figured you'd be on top of that," the caller said, "you always seemed to know everything when you were covering crime."

"Thanks," said Easton.

"But I think there's something you might not know, 'cause Gayle told me she hadn't told anybody about it."

"What's that?"

"The reporter who interviewed her tried to bribe her."

Easton sat up and grabbed a pen and a notepad.

"You're right, I didn't know that. Tell me about it."

"I don't want to say more right now," said the caller, "but when I heard it the first thing I thought was 'Gary Easton should know about this.'"

"Why?"

"'Cause you're Chicago's crime fighter," the caller said, "but I don't trust telephones, you know? You never know who's listening, right? Could we meet, just you and me?"

Easton put down his pen, frowning.

"Listen, ma'am, I'm a busy man and—"

"Oh," said the caller, "I realize that. It's just that I really admire you and I do know something you'll want to hear. It's important, I promise."

"I'm sure it is, ma'am, but—"

"I know who the reporter is," she said.

Easton absorbed that.

"How?"

"My friend Gayle told me. If you have the name, you could expose this woman, maybe turn her over to the D.A.'s office, get her disbarred or whatever it is they do to reporters. I mean, it's just not right, a reporter trying to pay people to lie."

Easton picked up his pen and scrawled "this woman" and "turn *her* over."

"Okay," he said, "I'm interested. How about I buy you a cup of coffee later today? There's a nice diner not far from my office, we could meet there, my treat."

"Too public," said the caller. "I don't want anybody to know I'm involved in this."

Easton sighed and rolled his eyes to the ceiling.

"Do you have something in mind?"

"I can't meet you today, I'm afraid. I can't leave my job until 5:00 p.m., 5:30 p.m. I'm on my break right now, at a pay phone around the corner from where I work. Could we meet tomorrow morning?"

"Saturday?"

"Yes. Someplace nice and quiet, just the two of us, right? I don't want to be exposed to anybody else, Gary. You're the only one I trust."

"Okay. Where would you like to meet?"

"Do you know the Baha'i Temple in Winnetka? It's a big white building, very pretty and tall. I'll be on the steps there tomorrow at nine o'clock in the morning."

"That's too early for me," said Easton. "I mean, Saturday's my day off unless there's something big happening. I like to sleep in."

"Of course," said the caller, "how thoughtless of me. You're important and you need your rest. Would ten o'clock be better?"

"Yes, that's good."

"Wonderful," she said. "I'll meet you on the steps, tomorrow at ten o'clock."

"How will I know you?"

"I'll wear my White Sox cap. I'm about five feet, five inches, my hair's kind of auburn. My favorite purse is bright red, I'll bring it."

"Got it," said Easton. "I'll see you there."

"Goody!"

"One more thing, ma'am."

"What's that?"

"This had better be good. If you're wasting my time, I won't be happy about it."

"Oh, you don't have to worry about that," she said, "I've got her name and enough detail about what she said to make the story stand up."

"Good," said Easton, "and goodbye."

When he arrived at the Temple, he understood why his caller had picked it. The imposing white structure was set well back from the street with an entry staircase which offered an unobstructed view of the street and anyone approaching the building. Easton climbed out of his car and walked toward the stairs, glancing left and right every few steps. He saw no one on the stairs and assumed his informant was inside the Temple, waiting behind the closed doors.

When he reached the top of the staircase, still checking left and right as he went, he spotted a plain white envelope. He drew closer to it and leaned over. His name was printed in squared block letters.

He picked it up and tore the flap open, extracting a single sheet of plain white paper. On it, in the same child-like block letters. It said:

Have Fun in Winnetka, Easton?

Across the street, Emily and Nikki Stone were hunkered down in Stone's ordinary Honda sedan, low enough to be obscure but just high enough to maintain their watch on the stairs. K.B. Constantine was in the back seat, slouched low against a door.

The three women watched Easton read the note, hold it to one side and spin around, glaring. He saw no one and held the note up again, reading it once more.

He balled the piece of paper and the envelope up—crushing both with more force than was necessary—and threw them to the pavement. He paused for a moment and then stomped on the ball of paper, crushing it until it was nearly flat. They were too far away from him to hear him, but they saw him raise his head to the sky and bellow something.

"I'll bet that wasn't a nice thing to say," said K.B.

"I imagine you're right," said Emily. "Great job, Nikki."

"I have to say, I'm surprised he actually showed up. I wasn't sure I'd convinced him."

"The combination of a little flattery, an appealing lie and the male ego," said Emily, "can go a long, long way."

They watched Easton stride rapidly down the stairs. He jerked his car door open and jumped in, slamming it behind him. The car fired up and Easton cut the wheel hard, making a U-turn with the gas pedal to the floor; the sharp turn generated a noisy screech and left a healthy portion of rubber on the pavement. When his car was out of sight, all three women started to giggle; it quickly grew into raucous laughter.

That evening, the Goods pulled into the short

circular driveway in front of the Winters' condo building. Emily and Ben climbed into the back seat.

"So, where to?" said Emily.

"Close by, one hopes," said Ben, "I'm quite peckish."

Greg swiveled around. "Sorry, my friend, but you'll have to hang on for a little while. We're driving out of town. Alicia insisted on it."

"Out of town? Where?"

"Glenview," said Alicia.

"What? That's absurd," said Ben.

"No, it's not," said Emily. "Good call, my friend."

"I knew you'd approve," said Alicia. She tapped her husband on the shoulder. "Take us away, good sir."

Ben sat back in his seat.

"Will someone enlighten me?"

Emily grinned. "If we're going to Glenview, then we are without question going to dine at Hackney's. It can't be anything else."

"Bingo," said Alicia.

They drove out of town and eventually arrived at the rural, woodsy location. The restaurant was quite busy. Ben eyed the small group of patrons awaiting their seats and scowled.

"One hopes, with considerable fervor, that one's dear friends had the foresight to secure a reservation."

Alicia smiled.

"They don't take them on weekends, Ben."

"Oh," said Ben, "this grows more tedious by the moment."

Greg held up both hands and grinned.

"Only until you get your burger," he said. "After which, your troubles will melt away like April snow."

Once seated and served, the couples spent the evening in energetic conversation. Ben and Greg traded some legal gossip. Ben's firm was coping with a few summer interns who were earnest and eager even if they were neophytes; Greg reported that he was struggling to select a new staff attorney from among several, each highly skilled and all enthusiastic, if not star struck, about ACLU's work.

Emily happily shared her payback moment and the four laughed heartily at the spectacle of Gary Easton hoist by his own petard.

"And while all this was going on," said Greg, "what were you up to, my friend."

"Ah," said Ben, "I was engaged in far more prosaic endeavors. The laundry had to be done, the guest bathroom needed a thorough cleaning and the filters in the air conditioners changing."

"How exciting," said Alicia, laughing.

"Truth be told," said Ben, "I enjoyed every moment of it. No chore can be mundane so long as one has one's music to enhance the experience."

Greg leaned forward.

"Hear anything good?"

"Heard nothing bad," said Ben. "Whilst folding the laundry, I devoured Muddy Water's "Mannish Boy," Randy Newman's "Short People," the Kinks' "Life Goes On," the Clash, Clapton, the Ramones and the Police."

"Quite the array," said Greg.

"Superior, in my view," said Ben, "all the more so for what was not among the lineup."

Emily laughed.

"He means there wasn't any disco," she said. "My guy hates it more than he hates improperly folded laundry."

"Far more indeed," said Ben. "Infinitely more."

"You guys are way ahead of me," said Alicia. "I haven't heard of half those bands. Were you using your turntable, Ben?"

"That came later in the day," he said. "I had the stereo tuned to 'XRT."

"What's that?"

"'XRT is Chicago's most delightful radio station. Adventuresome, eclectic, thoughtful, open-minded and, dare I say it, intelligent."

"Never heard of it," said Alicia.

Greg turned to her.

"Really? I'll put it on on the way home. It's very cool."

Alicia turned to Emily.

"You know about this, I suppose?"

Emily wasn't paying any attention. Her gaze had drifted up into the trees surrounding the dining patio and she kept it there.

"Emily? Are you here?"

Emily turned to look at her friend with a quizzical look.

"I'm sorry," she said, "Something just clicked."

"What?"

"The letters. Ben used three letters."

Ben took her hand and met her eyes.

"You do realize you're not making much sense," he said. "Has the wine blurred the lines?"

Emily smiled.

"'XRT,'" she said. "Three letters. X. R. T."

"It's the station I was listening to," said Ben, "you've heard it. I'm of the impression that you like it."

"I do," said Emily, "but that's not the point."

"I am ever more perplexed," said Ben. "What are you on about?"

"CCC," said Emily.

"What?"

"CCC. The guy who shot you. The guy who ran away, across the street and down Wellington."

"Perplexity squared," said Ben. "You're not making a scintilla of sense, m'love."

"Oh, yes I am," said Emily, her face bright and keen. "When you said 'XRT,' it came back to me, clear and certain. The guy was wearing a tee shirt and it had three letters on the back, bright red letters. CCC."

"So what?"

"Only this, dear. It's the first good lead I've had since NWCC was blown up."

Chapter Eighteen

"So it all comes together, Bert," said Emily. "Jon Haskill owns Consolidated Container Company, three C's. Ben wasn't the target when he got shot, I was, just like that shot at Uncle Max's cab in the driveway at the station. The shooter in the park was trying to hit me and he was wearing a tee shirt which had CCC in bright red letters."

"So it was Haskill?" Bert Presley shook his head. "I just don't see a CEO loading up a weapon and taking shots at a reporter."

"I don't think Haskill was the shooter, Bert. I'm guessing somebody who works for him or is close enough to have one of those tee shirts did it. We know Haskill's a major contributor to Right to Life Chicago; we know they were out to shut down the clinic. And he was angry with me when I tried to confront him—he literally ran away from me, which suggests that they really don't want me covering this story. Doesn't it make sense that he'd try to scare me off?"

"If he's the bomber, sure. He'd want you to stop investigating. But it's a giant leap from a tee shirt to where you land. Not enough there, Emily. It's too tenuous."

"For now," she said. "But when I confront him with the accusation, it's going to be tough for him to ignore it. At the very least, I could go on the air reporting that the person who shot at me twice and hit Ben the second time has direct ties to Haskill's company."

"Not without more than you've got right now," said Bert. "It's too thin. Of course, Haskill doesn't know that, does he?"

Emily laughed.

"Nope. He has no reason to believe that I won't air it and I can't think of any reason to tell him that you're such a stickler for facts."

"You play poker?"

"No. Why?"

"Because you're talking about running a serious bluff past this guy. I hope you can pull it off."

"We won't know until try, will we?"

"No. Okay, give it a go."

"Thanks. I'll go over to his building this morning."

"Fine. One more thing, Winter."

"What?"

"Take Constantine with you, right?"

"Of course."

"Good. I'd hate to give this guy a third shot at you."

"Me, too."

Emily pushed the buzzer at the entrance to Consolidated Container Company. K.B. Constantine was at her side and Scott Kern stood behind them.

"How can I help you?" The speaker crackled when the woman answered the buzzer.

"Good morning, ma'am. I'm Emily Winter, WSMP Team Eight News. I have some questions for Mr. Haskill."

"About what?"

"About the bombing of the Northside Women's Care Clinic and his role in trying to cover it up."

"Sorry. He doesn't talk to the press."

"I'm aware of that," said Emily, "but I think he will want to see me. I have reason to believe that he, or someone associated with your company, is guilty of attempted murder."

"What? That's absurd."

"The evidence suggests it is not, ma'am. Could you please just let him know I'm here and I want to hear his side of the story before we put it on the air?"

"You mean, on the TV?"

"Yes, ma'am."

"Oh dear. Wait there, please."

A few minutes passed and the buzzer crackled again.

"There's a loading dock, down at the other end of the building, around the corner. Mr. Haskill will meet you there."

The three walked to the corner of the building. When they reached it, K.B. held up a hand and stopped Emily and Scott.

"Wait here," she said. "I want to have a look first."

She turned the corner and stood, perfectly still, surveying the area. There was a large paved area holding several medium sized company trucks in a line and one backed up to the loading dock. K.B. took a step back and leaned around the corner of the building.

"I need you two to walk slowly. I'm going to circle around the parked trucks and then I'll join you. Don't go near the dock until I'm back in sight, okay?"

"Got it," said Kern.

K.B. moved rapidly, her eyes scanning the area over and over. Emily and Scott strolled toward the loading dock. Halfway there, Scott paused to adjust his camera's shoulder strap; a few steps later, Emily stopped to bend down and retie a shoelace. When Constantine emerged from behind the last truck in the line, they picked up the pace.

Jon Haskill was standing on the edge of the dock. Several workers were moving boxes from a forklift to the truck bed while the driver watched and a young man with a clipboard checked off the boxes as they moved into the truck. Two of the workers, the driver and the young man, were wearing tee shirts; Emily and Scott both confirmed that the shirts had red letters on the backs—CCC.

Jon Haskill walked down a short set of stairs and met them on the tarmac. He was well dressed and he took care as he moved to avoid brushing against the walls or the boxes strewn on the dock.

"I believe I told you that I have nothing to say to you. That hasn't changed. Tell your man there that if he turns on that camera, I'll have you removed from the property. We clear on that?"

"No camera," said Emily. "For now."

"Who's this?"

K.B. had joined them.

"She's a WSMP intern, sir, a grad student at Northwestern. She's just here to observe."

"Three of you? This is ridiculous. You actually think somebody in my shop is trying to murder somebody?"

"I don't think it, sir. I know it. And there's more—the shooter hit someone. My husband Ben was wounded."

"And how is that connected to my business?"

"The shooter was wearing one of those shirts," said Emily, pointing to the nearest worker.

Haskill looked at the worker and then burst into laughter.

"That's it? That's what you've got? That's just ridiculous."

"I don't find any humor in this, Mr. Haskill."

"I'm sure you don't, but I do."

"How?"

"Listen, young lady. Two years ago, for our fifteenth anniversary, we ordered those shirts. Would you care to guess how many?"

Emily frowned. "Several dozen?"

Haskill laughed again.

"The cost per unit dropped, the more we ordered. We bought seven hundred fifty of them."

"I see."

"No, I don't think you do. We gave one to each

employee. We held a company picnic that year, over in Grant Park. Everybody brought their families. We gave tee shirts to everyone who was there, kids, wives, boyfriends, girlfriends. We still had several hundred left, so we started using them as a marketing tool. We gave some to our regular customers. We took them to a food manufacturer convention at McCormick and gave everybody who stopped at our display table a shirt or two. I gave a bunch to the rec center next door to my church. There's a rec league basketball team at the center, we gave the players shirts, too. Did that two years running and I've still got a couple boxes of the damn things in a storage closet."

"I see," said Emily, trying not to let her disappointment show. "Still,—"

"No, young lady, there's no 'still' about it. Hundreds of people have those shirts, scattered all over the city and, for that matter, all over the Midwest. This shooter you're talking about may have worn one, but there's no way you can prove any connection between that fact, if it's even true, and my company."

Haskill turned and took two steps up the stairs. He turned back, looking down at Emily, and sneered.

"I have nothing more to say to you. Your theory is impossible to prove; you've got nothing but tee shirts to connect me or Consolidated Container to the shootings. I'll ask you to leave the property now. And that camera stays off or you'll hear from my attorney. Leave. Now."

"He's right, you know," said Kern as he loaded his gear into the back of the station's wagon. "So many shirts, we've got no way to know who had one. Even if it was one of his shirts, we have no way of knowing who wore it. One of his workers? Some teenager? A total stranger? Sorry, Emily, I just don't think there's anything to work with here. Nice try, but it's a dead end."

Emily climbed in the front seat of the wagon and turned to face K.B.

"What do you think?"

Constantine shrugged.

"I think Scott's right."

"But, it's so obvious, isn't it? I mean, there's a direct connection between the shirts and Haskill's beliefs about NWCC's work. I'm sure he's involved."

Emily sighed and turned, staring out the window.

"Well, I noticed something else," said K.B.

"What?"

"Did you look past the loading dock?"

"No. I saw those guys on the dock, wearing those shirts, and figured that was that. Why? What else was there to see?"

"Beyond the boxes. There are assembly lines and conveyor belts."

"So what?"

"Bottles," said Constantine. "Hundreds, maybe thousands, of bottles back there, coming off the lines and running down the conveyor belts. I saw at least three different versions. Bottles the size of a mayonnaise or pickle jar, bottles big enough to hold a gallon of milk or water or whatever and big bottles, I'd say five, maybe six gallons."

Emily nodded.

"And if you're going to make a Molotov cocktail—"

"Exactly. First thing you need, you need big glass bottles."

"Which you can buy at any grocery store on earth," said Kern. "They may be filled with stuff when they come off the shelf, but if you pour what's in there out and replace it with gasoline—"

"You've got a fire bomb," said Emily. "So even if the tee shirts don't lead us anywhere, maybe the bottles do."

"And maybe not," said Kern. "Looks to me, Winter, like you're all bottled up."

Emily gave him a look and groaned.

Kern grinned. "Can we stop for lunch on the way back? I'm starving."

They rode toward the station in silence. Emily stared out the window all the way, turning it all over. By the time they found a lunch spot, she was so distraught that she thought she might cry.

"Well," said K.B., "it was a good theory. Too bad it didn't play out."

"It still could," said Emily. "I'm convinced he's involved."

"Why?"

"For one thing, he never said I was wrong," said

Emily. "He just said I can't prove it."

"I'll give you that," said Kern, "but you still come up empty."

"Maybe so," said Emily, "but now I've got something to work with."

"What's that?"

"Tee shirts," said Emily. "Lots and lots of tee shirts."

"Good luck making the connection," said Kern. "In the meantime, let's eat. Looks like this little mall has two choices. Burgers or deli?"

"Deli," said Emily.

"Ditto," said K.B.

"I was so sure," said Emily. "I was certain the shirt was a solid lead."

"It still is, is it not?" said Ben.

"Hundreds of them? I don't see how I'll ever make the connection. They're scattered all over the place. I don't see how I can run down the only one that matters."

"Gracious," said Ben. "That's a new wrinkle."

"What is?"

"You, sounding discouraged. I don't believe I've ever—no, that's not accurate. I cannot recall the last time I heard you consider the possibility of defeat."

"Not exactly a momentous milestone, is it?"

"You do yourself a disservice."

They were at the dining table, working on a pizza

and nursing cold beers.

"You're sweet to say so," said Emily, "but I just don't see this panning out."

"Perhaps not," said Ben, "but would you have me believe that if the tee shirt doesn't solve the case, you're done?"

"No, not that, exactly. I'm just stuck, Ben. I don't know where to go. I was so sure, but it's clear I was wrong. Or if I'm right, I can't prove it."

"Perhaps. Perhaps not. You did secure valuable grist for the mill, you know."

"What?"

"The bottles, for one thing. K.B. could be right about that, that CCC may be the source of the raw material for a firebomb. And, did you not tell me that he never denied your core theory? He gloated that you could not prove it, but he did not deny it. Isn't that worth considering?"

"I suppose, but I still don't see where it leads me. He certainly isn't going to call me in the morning and confess. And Carol Lobes and Norman Brent still won't talk to me. Sam Terhune is in Connecticut; there's no way he was out there in the park shooting at us."

She gazed out the window and took a sip of beer.

"If I sound discouraged, Ben, it's because I am."

"This is not a new experience, you know. You've been in such a quandary before, confronting an investigation which appears to be without resolution."

"Yes, but—"

Ben set his slice aside and held up a hand, stopping her.

"No. I shan't accept any 'but.' You've faced stonewalls before and, without fail, you have climbed them, maneuvered around them, found another path. If you can't find a crack in the wall, you create one. You're a capable, skillful reporter, m'love. You may be at loggerheads at this moment, but you've always found a way and you will do so again."

"I don't know how," she said.

"Piffle! You know how to investigate, you know how to interview, you know how to find a lead and follow it. You are a reporter, Emily, and at least one of those to whom you report believes there is none better in this fair city."

"You're biased."

"Be that as it may. I am also a discerning consumer of news, so I know whereof I speak. And, need I note, I am not alone. Two highly reputable news directors know firsthand how talented you are. Dean Lyon, when you were writing morning news for the El, Bert Presley at WSMP. They are not fools, as you well know, and they have full faith and confidence in your prowess."

"Thanks," she said.

"So, there remains but one path to follow, yes?"

"What's that?"

"You're a reporter, m'love. Go report."

"Okay," she said, "but not tonight. Tonight, I want to polish off this slice and turn on the TV. I want to watch something stupid and silly."

"A goal easily attained," said Ben. "Just as you are at your best when you're determined to cover a story, the networks are at their best when it comes to stupid and silly. You go turn on the set. I'm going to rinse these dishes and I'll join you anon. Would you like another beer?"

Emily smiled.

"No," she said. "If I'm going to be reporting first thing tomorrow, I want to be sharp."

"Capital," said Ben. "Outstanding."

Chapter Nineteen

With a vending machine tuna fish sandwich and an iced tea, Emily sat at her desk and considered Ben's admonition—"when you can't find a crack in the wall you create one." She looked over her notes, seeking anything which looked like an opening. She made a short list of possibilities and moved her phone to the middle of her desk.

In between nibbles, she called Sam Terhune's home and spoke to his mother, confirming that Sam was indeed in Connecticut and that she didn't have a number where he could be reached because "he doesn't exactly have a place to stay yet—the dorms aren't open."

She called Norman Brent and got his answering machine. She didn't dial Jon Haskill's office because she knew it would be futile.

The remaining possibility on her list was Carol Lobes. Before she dialed that number, she sat back to finish her sandwich and thought about how to navigate the call if Lobes answered her phone. It took some time, but eventually she had a strategy in mind.

"Hello?"

"Hi, Mrs. Lobes, this is Emily Winter."

"You again? You know I can't—"

"You can't talk about the investigation into the bombing. Yes, I know that. I'm calling for a different reason."

"What?"

"I need your help."

"Me? Whatever for?"

"Somebody's trying to kill me, Mrs. Lobes. The police haven't been able to figure out who, so I'm trying to sort it out on my own."

"That's horrible. Are you serious?"

"I am. Twice, somebody has shot at me. I can't go anywhere without a bodyguard. The second attempt missed me, but it hit my husband. He's going to be okay, but only because we were lucky."

"I'm sorry. That must be frightening—"

"Very."

"—but I can't imagine how I can help. What does this have to do with me?"

"I can only think of one reason that somebody's shooting at me, Mrs. Lobes. I haven't stopped investigating the bombing at the clinic and I'm pretty sure somebody is trying to scare me off."

"Well, I don't know anything about—"

"Mrs. Lobes, please just hear me out. When we have talked before—on your picket line and then in your living room—you made it clear that you fight for what you believe to be right. I have no doubt that your work for RTLC is sincere and honest because your religious beliefs tell you that it's wrong to take a life. That's why you give RTLC so much of your time, it's why you were on the picket line, it's why you went to court."

"Yes. Of course. But—"

"I admire that, your faith in your church's teachings about what's right and wrong."

"I still don't see—"

"You are certain that it's wrong to take a life and it's your, what, your duty, your calling, to prevent that. Isn't that right?"

"Yes."

"Including mine? Or my husband's?"

"Certainly. Killing is wrong, it's a sin."

"And you're dedicated to preventing that sin if you can."

"I am."

"Well, if I'm right, if somebody is intent on killing me—"

"Mrs. Winter, I don't know anything about that."

"Are you sure? Can you think of anybody in your group who might be angry enough to take drastic action? Maybe you've heard somebody say something, or threaten to do something?"

Lobes didn't speak. Her silence continued and Emily fought down the impulse to fill the emptiness in the conversation. *Let it percolate,* she thought, *she's more uncomfortable with the silence than I am.* Emily shifted in her seat, fidgeted with her sandwich wrapper, tapped her pen on her desk, waiting. Just before she couldn't stand it any longer, Lobes spoke, her voice quiet and, Emily thought, just a little shaky.

"I can't help you. I'm sorry."

"Please, Mrs. Lobes—"

The line went dead.

"We have to try, Scott. I don't have anything else to work with. We're already here, let's just go knock on his door. Maybe he'll answer."

"You're nuts," said Kern. "Norman Brent? Last time you tried this, he wouldn't even open the door."

They were heading back to the studio to edit a series of interviews Emily had conducted with holocaust survivors who were furious—and frightened—about a proposed demonstration by neo-Nazis in Skokie, their hometown. The survivors had been passionately expressive; Emily had drawn them out and she and Scott both came away from the synagogue knowing they had some highly dramatic and compelling material to air that night. Still, as soon as they were done with the last interview, Emily's thoughts turned immediately to the NWCC story.

"We don't have your bodyguard," said Scott. "I'm not all that comfortable confronting this guy without her."

K.B. Constantine had swept through the synagogue where the interviews had taken place and had a stern conversation with the building's security guard. Having satisfied herself that the location was safe, she left them. They all agreed that they would meet back at the station.

"We could call her," said Emily, "or we can give it a go and figure that, even if he's the shooter, Brent won't do anything stupid when you've got a camera on him."

"By 'stupid,' you mean take a shot at you? You are nuts. He's that crazy, you think he'd stop with you and let me walk away? I got Cubs tickets this weekend, pal. I plan to use them, it's okay with you."

Emily chuckled, but she didn't want to give up.

"How about this? We go to his apartment building, we check the parking lot. They have designated spaces, remember? We saw that when we were there last time. If his car isn't in his space, we go back to the studio. If it is, you use that two-way radio thing, check in with the office and let K.B. know what we're up to. I even promise to wait for her before we knock on his door."

Kern waited until they hit a red light, then turned to face her.

"Don't you ever give up?"

"Nope."

"We don't go near his door unless K.B.'s with us?"

"I promise."

He sighed.

"I gotta be out of my mind."

He wheeled the station wagon and turned,

heading for Norman Brent's home.

Brent's parking space was empty.

"Sorry, pal," said Kern, "no go."

"I see," she said. "Okay, I give up. Let's get back and edit the stuff we got. At least Bert's going to be happy—they gave us really compelling stuff."

"We need gas," said Kern.

They went down the block from Brent's building and pulled into a MidAm gas station. Emily went inside and bought two candy bars while Kern filled the tank.

"Take your pick," she said, "I'm cranky and annoyed and tired. Chocolate is the only thing's going to help. I'm happy with either of these. Which one you want?"

"Snickers," said Kern.

"Good choice," she said.

While Kern topped off the tank, Emily got in the wagon and tore open her Three Musketeers. She took a sizable bite and gazed absently out the window, chewing and watching as a car pulled into the station. The car passed under the MidAm sign and Emily stared at it for a moment.

"Is that candy bar that good?" asked Kern when he climbed in.

"Huh?"

"You got a big ole grin on your face," he said. "What's so funny?"

Emily looked at him, her eyes sparkling.

"Not funny," she said. "Just a very devious idea."

—————

"So, you don't need me anymore?"

Uncle Max looked at Emily with a mixture of disappointment and confusion.

"Max, you know you're my main guy, always have been, always will be. But after we got shot at, Ben said I had to have protection so we hired—well, we and the station—hired a cop who's on leave."

Max shifted his gaze from Emily to his nephew.

"What, I'm not good enough?"

Ben smiled.

"You're the best, Uncle, the *ne plus ultra*. I wanted somebody who's well-trained and armed—you wouldn't want me taking any chances with our Emily, would you?"

"I don't know about that knee stuff," said Max, "but I'm a pretty tough cookie, comes down to it. I was all over that bozo, the one runs the container company." He turned back to Emily. "I handled him, right?"

"You were the very picture of a tough guy, Max, and I love you for that. But, you have to admit, this is different. Besides, we all think the shooter is after me, so if you're my driver, that puts you in the line of fire. If anything happened to you, Max, I'd never forgive myself."

Max blushed.

"Aw, geez, Emmy."

"So, Max," said Ben, "you surely must acknowledge that, just until this matter comes to fruition, it's best for all if you're safe and Emily is, too."

Max frowned and then nodded once.

"Okay, I get it. Can't say I like it, but I get it. One thing, though."

"What?"

"Soon as this crap is over, I'm back on the job, right?"

Emily and Ben laughed.

"Absolutely," said Emily.

"Without doubt," said Ben.

"Damn straight," said Max. He turned and started his cab, wheeling it out of the driveway. "I'm gonna put a little extra on the pedal, you don't mind. Cousin Debby's fixin' her killer pasta and we're already runnin' late."

"Full speed ahead," said Ben. "We dare not threaten your access to Debby's artful cuisine."

Ben took Emily's hand.

"So, you're still up against the wall?"

"I am," she said. "I thought I'd broken through with Carol Lobes, but she hung up on me. There was a hint of something in her voice, but I don't think I can persuade her to talk. Norman Brent wasn't home. Jon Haskill's out of the question, at least when it comes to me."

"Tell me again what Mrs. Lobes said."

"She said 'I can't help you.'"

Ben's gaze drifted out the window for a moment.

"Not 'I won't' but 'I can't'?"

"Yes. Are you thinking what I am?"

"Perhaps. 'Won't' implies that she refuses. 'Can't'

suggests that she may know something but is unable to speak."

"Exactly. I thought she was uncomfortable, maybe reluctant. Of course, that could be me, desperate to find anything, anything at all, to break this thing open."

"Or you could be right," said Ben. "Were I you, I'd give it some thoughtful scrutiny."

"We're here," said Max. "Everybody out."

Ben's family greeted them warmly and the group—some twelve of them—dined on a meal which drew raves and included hearty conversation which was as familiar, as entertaining and as relaxed as only cordial family gatherings can be.

Hours later, Max drove them home. He put on the radio and they listened to WFMT's Midnight Special—the station's celebrated once a week departure from classical music. Ben provided a running commentary on the eclectic music they heard. Emily listened, but not intently, staring out the window as Chicago rolled by. As they pulled into the driveway, Emily turned to Ben, her eyes sharply focused.

"What?"

"She has to be protecting somebody," said Emily.

"A reference to Mrs. Lobes, I trust."

"Of course. Either she's protecting somebody or she's scared. Nothing else makes sense."

Emily and Ben spent the next day luxuriating in a lazy day, sleeping late, consuming Sunday newspapers, enjoying breakfast and snacks. They took a long walk in the sunny park, the humidity at a reasonable level and the temperature a few degrees below ninety. Ben was still using his walking stick, even though his limp was barely discernible, the wound on his leg no longer bandaged. For the first few blocks, Emily was wary, checking over her shoulder, looking behind trees, watching the light traffic for signs of danger. Eventually, she began to relax and on the return trek, she held her husband's hand and allowed herself to simply enjoy the walk, his company and a lovely summer day.

It wasn't until they were in bed, right on the edge of sleep, that the idea came to her.

Forget about the people, she thought, *concentrate on the killer cocktail.*

Chapter Twenty

When the Monday morning planning meeting broke up, Emily scurried around the conference table and tapped Don Malafronte on the shoulder.

"Hi, Emily. What's up?"

"I need a favor," she said.

"From me?"

"Yes. You may have access to something I need. Or, to be fair, something I think I need."

"What would that be?"

When she told him, he grinned.

At her desk, Emily rifled through her Rolodex and found Linda Marshall's office number.

"Linda, it's Emily."

"Hi! I've been thinking of you—the Rules Committee has met twice in a row without you, we all wondered about that. Everything okay?"

"Yes. Well, almost everything. The NWCC case has been driving me crazy and I'm still feeling edgy about the shooter—"

"Ben's all better now?"

"I think so, the doctor thinks so and his limp is

entirely gone. The stitches fell out over the weekend."

"Well, that's good news. Did you call to make a lunch date? I'd love that."

"In a manner of speaking. I need a favor. Can you do some digging for me?"

"Sure. What's up?"

"I need to know more about a business. I won't go into details, but I can't go directly to them. I don't work that beat, but you do. You'll know where to look and who to ask and it would take me weeks to do it. I don't think what I'm after should be difficult. Would you mind?"

"My pleasure."

Emily described what she needed. Linda Marshall took a few notes.

"This should be easy," she said. "Let's do this. We'll meet for lunch day after tomorrow, I should have most of what you're after by then."

"See? I was right. You can do it in a couple of days, I'd take that long just figuring out how to get started. It's a date. Any thoughts on where to meet?"

"How about R. J. Grunt's?"

"That'd be fun," said Emily. "Let's make it 11:30 a.m., maybe beat the lunch rush by a few minutes. See you then and there."

"Great."

Emily entered the date in her notepad and dialed the phone again.

"Chicago Fire. How may I direct your call?"

"Can you connect me with Sean Sheehan, please?"

"Arson investigation."

"May I speak with Mr. Sheehan?"

"Who's calling?"

"Emily Winter, WSMP News."

"Hold on."

"This is Sean."

"Hi, Mr. Sheehan. I don't know if you remember—"

"You were on the scene at the clinic bombing. You're the one, broke the news about the Molotov Cocktail."

"Right."

"How can I help you?"

"I've got some questions I'm hoping you can answer."

"Shoot."

"First, am I correct that you and your team gathered a lot of physical evidence after the fire?"

"Bags full. We did a bunch of lab work to confirm what we thought—no doubt that it was two firebombs, both through the front windows, one on each side of the place. We know gasoline was the cause—ordinary gas, you can buy it at any station in town. We've got shards and photos; the thing comes to trial, we can testify how the fire started, how it spread, the damage it did and the only plausible cause of death."

"And it's still available? I mean, you're still treating it as an open case?"

"Of course. That all?"

"No, not quite. If somebody came up with a theory about the origin of the cocktails, how they were made, the materials used, could your team verify that?"

"That's a little vague, but, it's certainly possible that we could match physical evidence to a theory. I can't be sure, of course, until we know what we're looking for. Can you be more specific?"

"Not yet," said Emily, "I'm still chasing down leads."

"You working with the cops?"

"I've been in touch with Jack Potter all along, although neither of us has come up with anything solid yet, but if my leads pan out, he's the first person I'll contact. I'll work with the homicide team if the time comes."

"Good. I don't want this case to get blown up because somebody interfered with the official investigation. Whoever did this should be locked up for a long, long time; we need to dot all the i's and cross all the t's. I'd hate to see a jury tainted or evidence thrown out."

"Not to worry," said Emily, "I want justice, too. Thanks for your help."

"Not sure I helped, but you're welcome."

"One more thing," said Emily.

"What?"

"You don't want the 'case to get blown up.' Is that pun intentional?"

Sheehan laughed.

"Nope."

"Never mind," said Emily, "I'll share it with my husband anyhow. He'll love it."

———————

Emily ordered the grilled two-cheese sandwich, Linda Marshall, the bacon cheeseburger. They ordered an Oreo milkshake served in two glasses so they could share it.

"This was easy," said Marshall. "I got the basics. Years in business, corporation filings, management roster, several years of P & L, customer base."

"P & L?"

"Profit and loss. In this case, it's just profit. The place is well-managed, they've got a solid sales team, an impressive number of long-term clients. They've been turning a profit from the get-go."

"I don't think I need any of the financial stuff," said Emily.

"Just in case." Marshall slid a file folder across the table. "It's all here."

"Thanks. What I'm really after is customers."

"There's a list in there, current to about six months ago."

Their order arrived and they eagerly ate. Marshall had onion rings with her burger, Emily had fries; they shared both the sides equally as they shared idle work chatter, too. Emily related her encounter with Gary Easton. Linda thought it was as hilarious as it was justified. Marshall brought Emily up to date on gossip from the most recent Rules Committee gatherings. The handsome new anchor at Mary Massey's station had, in fact, moved back to D.C.; Lois Lipton had been assigned to cover court developments surrounding the proposed neo-Nazi demonstration in Skokie. They both agreed that Lipton had, at last, secured a front page assignment and Marshall reported that the Committee had engineered a proper celebration—"We didn't let Lois buy a drink all night."

When the lunch ended, Emily made a call and waited, just inside the doors to the restaurant, until Uncle Max's cab appeared on the corner. Emily walked briskly to the car and climbed in the back seat; K.B. Constantine was in the front seat beside Max.

"Thanks for the ride, Max."

"My pleasure. You didn't tell me this young lady was such a babe, Emily. Plus, we've been talking about the Cubs, she knows her baseball."

"Max, she is a fully-trained police officer, a crack shot and she's so quick on her feet you wouldn't believe it. I don't think 'babe' is exactly respectful, you know?"

"Aw, lighten up, wouldja? I was payin' her a compliment."

Max turned to glance at K.B.

"No offense, ma'am."

K.B. smiled.

"None taken, sir. Trust me when I tell you, 'babe' is a hanging curveball compared to what they call me in the station house."

"Yeah? That's dumb. Way I see it, you broads ought to be allowed to do whatever you're good enough to do. I been tellin' Emily that for years now."

"And I've been doing my best to get you to give up on 'broads' and 'babes' for at least that long, Max. You're dealing with two of us now, right? You're outnumbered and between us, we'll make a feminist out of you yet."

"Maybe so," said Max, "but you tell my buddies in the garage that, I'll never live it down."

"It'll be our secret," said K.B.

"Not entirely," said Emily. "You make the grade, Max, I'm telling Benjamin."

"You'd do that?"

"In a hot minute," said Emily, "but I wouldn't worry about it just yet."

"Why not?"

"I love you to pieces, Max, and I know you're trying, but you're not there yet."

"Broads," said Max, "a fella can't win for losin.'"

Emily spent the balance of the day at the station, helping Scott Kern and Nikki Stone edit film of an encounter with Steve Dahl, the DJ who had been fired in the aftermath of his "Disco Demolition Night" which had generated mayhem and controversy at Comiskey Park. Dahl had been out of work for a month and Stone had secured a very good interview in which Dahl, while unrepentant, had energetically reflected on the event and its aftermath. They spliced the interview with tape of the explosive evening into a segment which Emily and Scott thought certain to draw larger than ordinary ratings. To make sure, they edited two short promos which included the scene at Comiskey and Stone's "EXCLUSIVE" interview.

On the way home, Emily had K.B. stop at a local supermarket. With K.B. at her side, Emily prowled the aisles until she found several specific items—a container of grape jelly, a jar of dill pickles and another of Greek olives, and a gallon of distilled water.

K.B. walked Emily to the door of the condo and confirmed that Ben was at home before she went home for the evening.

"Are we out of olives?"

"I don't have any idea," said Emily.

"Then, why—"

"Because I need them," said Emily.

"For what, pray tell?"

"Research."

"And grape jelly? Do we not have a sufficient supply in the fridge?"

"Probably."

"So, our supply of pickles and jelly is sufficient and yet—"

"Do I smell chicken?"

"You do indeed, m'love. Lightly seasoned, broiling for crispness. There's a salad as well and watermelon is in season, so I added that to it. And fresh green beans."

"Sounds delicious," said Emily. "I'll set the table."

"Without explaining...wait, there's more? Why do we need distilled water?"

"All in good time, Benjamin. Right now, I'd like a glass of wine. How soon is dinner?"

"Ten, maybe twelve minutes."

"Pour me a glass. I'll change before I do the table."

On Thursday, Donald Malafronte walked into the newsroom and tapped on the partition at Emily's cubicle.

"I have what you need. It took some doing—they had to dig back to find it. You're lucky, they don't usually keep these around, at least not that far back. They were in a box in the storage room. They recycle them—erase what's there and start over—but they hadn't gotten around to it yet."

He held out a cardboard box which had a dozen or so smaller black cases in it.

"You wanted five days, right?"

"Exactly," said Emily.

"Well, these should cover it. They're all labeled, date and time."

"That's great, Donald. Thanks."

"Are they important?"

"I won't know until I've checked them out, but yes, if I find what I think I'm going to find, they're more than important. They're front-page news."

On Friday morning, an hour before the planning meeting, Emily walked into Bert Presley's office.

"I'd like to skip the meeting this morning," she said.

"Why?"

"I'm going to be in the editing bay, probably most of the day."

"Why?"

"I'm working on a theory."

"About what?"

"NWCC."

"Really? What have you got?"

"Maybe nothing, Bert. Maybe everything."

"Could you be more mysterious? What is this, twenty questions?"

"More like Clue."

"Colonel Mustard in the billiard room?"

"Something like that."

"And for this you skip our meeting? And, since you won't be there, you're skipping an assignment, too?"

"It's just one day, Bert."

"It better be worth it, Winter."

"I hope so."

Chapter Twenty-One

"So that's what I have," said Emily. "What I don't have is a way to tie it all together. I need one more piece and it's not going to be easy to get. I'm hoping you'll have an idea."

Bert Presley leaned his chair back and propped his feet up on his desk.

"You need an interview."

"At least one. Maybe two."

"There's only one I want."

"That's why I need your help. How do we make that happen?"

"We could kidnap him."

"I was hoping for something a bit more subtle."

"And legal."

"And legal. How can we set it up?"

"Play him."

"How?"

"What matters to him? What would get him to give up his silence?"

Emily nodded.

"That's easy. He hates choice. He doesn't believe

that women should be allowed any control over their own bodies if they are pregnant."

"Yup. We already know he'll go to great lengths to prevent abortions and harass anybody who thinks otherwise. So?"

"Let me think about it," said Emily.

"Do that. You know how."

"I do?"

"Sure you do. Just ask Gary Easton."

Emily's eyes widened and she blushed.

"You know about that?"

"Sooner or later, I hear it all. The grapevine around here is constantly active and rarely wrong. You snookered the guy—made me laugh when I heard it, by the way. Whatever guile you used then, use it now."

"Huh. I hadn't thought about it like that."

"Now you have."

———

Norman Brent worked behind the counter at an auto parts store. He was closing out a sale—a fan belt, a generator belt and windshield wipers for a 1970 Ford Falcon—when the phone rang.

"Chi-Town Auto Supply, front desk."

"Good morning. I'd like to speak to Norman Brent, please."

"Speaking."

"Mr. Brent, my name is Nikki Stone, I'm a WSMP reporter. I covered the hearing—"

"I have nothing to say to you."

"—the hearing when your group won the right to demonstrate in front of the Northwest Women's Care Clinic. Are you aware that they are planning to open a new facility?"

"I heard that, but—"

"Are you aware that they might go to court to prevent your group from demonstrating when the new clinic opens?"

"They can't do that. We already won, we're allowed."

"You were allowed, Mr. Brent. The clinic can argue that the bombing of their former clinic changed everything. Since their clinic was destroyed and their chief physician was killed, they may seek a permanent injunction against Right To Life Chicago. They could ask for it before the new clinic even opens."

"Nobody told us about this," said Brent. "How do you know?"

"We have our sources. The thing is, sir, we know you and your colleagues won't talk about the bombing, but will you give us a reaction to a request for a new injunction?"

"Hell, yes. We'll fight 'em in court, just like we did last time. We'll win, too. You can quote me."

"We'd like to go one better than that, sir. We'd like to interview you."

"On camera?"

"On camera. We can come to you or—"

"No. Not here. This place has nothing to do with

my work for RTLC, I don't want them involved. Besides, they'd probably can me."

"Well, we don't want that, do we? How about this? You can come to our studios, we'll do the interview here. When would be convenient for you?"

Brent hesitated. Stone held her tongue while Emily, sitting across the conference table, away from the speaker phone, held her breath.

"When are they going to court?"

"It could be soon. They've already laid the foundation for the new clinic, crews are working on it now. What would be best for us would be to have your reaction in the can so if they go to court, we can present your side. I guess you'd want that, too, right? You'll want to get your message out at the same time they do, won't you?"

"Yes. No doubt about it."

"Well, how about later today, or tomorrow if that's easier."

"I get a ninety-minute lunch break. Could we do it around 12:30?"

"We can arrange that for you. Do you have our address?"

"I know where you are."

"12:30, then. Thank you for cooperating. See you later."

Nikki ended the call before he could respond.

———

Scott Kern set up the camera at the far end of the

conference table. Emily set up chairs at the other end, arranging them so the interviewer and Brent would face one another. Between and behind the two chairs was a metal cart which contained a television set; the set was attached to a tape machine.

K.B. Constantine waited at the front desk and when Norman Brent arrived, she ushered him into the conference room.

Scott Kern moved from behind the camera. He extended his hand and said, "Mr. Brent, I'm Scott Kern, I'll be running the camera. You've met our intern, K.B. Constantine. She'll be working with me."

Kern shook Brent's hand and nodded to the occupied chair at the end of the table.

"What's she doing here?"

Emily, seated in one of the two interview chairs, stood up.

"I'm Emily Winter, Mr. Brent. But you already know that, don't you?"

He hesitated before he said, "You were at our demonstrations. I've seen you on the TV. You're not the one who called me."

"No, I'm not. That was Ms. Stone. She was called away to cover another assignment."

"So, what's—"

"Emily will be conducting the interview," said Kern.

"I thought it would be that other woman."

His voice cracked just a little and a distinct look of discomfort flashed across his face.

"Nope. The bosses want Emily to do it. Sorry if that's not what you expected, but, you know how bosses can be."

Brent didn't speak.

"Please," said Emily, gesturing to the empty chair, "join me."

He held his ground for a moment and then, warily, walked to her. Kern followed and attached a microphone to his shirt and went back to his rig.

"If you'll just say your name for me, sir, and spell it," said Kern, "I'll get a good level for the audio."

Without taking his eyes off Emily, Brent spoke, dropping his chin a little to get closer to the mic.

"No need to lean down, sir," said Kern. "The level's gonna be fine if you just speak normally. Just talk to Emily like you would to anybody else. Got it?"

"Yes."

"Okay, then. Rolling. Ready when you are, Emily."

"Mr. Norman Brent, just for identification, you are a co-chair of Right To Life Chicago?"

"I am, yes."

"Thank you. We're going to show you a short piece of videotape and then I'll ask you about it. Ready?"

"What tape?"

"You'll see. It's pretty self-explanatory."

Emily leaned over and switched the TV set on and then pushed the Play button on the recorder.

The picture was of poor quality, grainy black and white, harshly and poorly lit. It had been shot after dark, the camera was focused on an area below a bank of fluorescent lights.

Norman Brent sat bolt upright, his eyes flaring and his mouth agape.

"Where'd you get—"

"Just wait, Mr. Brent. And watch."

A man appeared under the lights. He was carrying a large container with a wide cap on one end and a spout on the other. He unscrewed the cap, lifted the nozzle from the pump and began filling the container with gasoline.

Brent rose from his chair.

"I'm not going to sit here and—"

Emily remained seated and spoke calmly.

"Mr. Brent, think carefully. We have the tape. We're going to air the tape. We have other evidence as well. You are certainly free to leave, but that will just force us to say that we showed this film to you and you refused to comment. I think you can imagine what the audience will think if they see the tape and then learn that you ran away from us. It won't look very good, will it?"

"You lied to me," he said, his voice harsh and rattled. "You told me—"

"We told you that NWCC might be planning to sue you again. That's not a lie. It could happen. It's true that we have another reason to talk to you, but we didn't lie."

Brent stood still, his eyes darting between the door and the TV set beside him. Emily waited, still seated and still calm. K.B. Constantine moved, taking rapid strides to the conference room door and standing, alert and poised for action, in front of the door.

"There's just a little more on the tape, sir," said Emily. "Why don't you just sit down and let it finish?"

Brent nodded numbly and sank into his seat. His balding scalp and forehead were damp with sweat and he licked his lips several times, trying without success to moisten them.

The figure on the screen returned the nozzle to its pump, bent over to grab the handle of the container and hoisted it. He walked to the back of his car and opened the trunk, dropped the container inside and moved toward the front seat. As he did so, he glanced at the pump and, in so doing, exposed his full face to the camera. For all its flaws, the tape left no doubt that the man who pumped the gas was Norman Brent.

When he reached the car door, he turned his back to the camera to climb in. The last shot the camera captured before he disappeared into his car was the back of his shirt. It displayed three large Cs.

Nikki Stone sat in the WSMP station wagon, waiting with a cameraman. They had parked the wagon in an empty spot in the Consolidated Container Company's lot, as close to Jon Haskill's space as they could get.

When the unmarked police car pulled into the

lot and parked in the aisle, blocking Haskill's Cadillac, Stone and the camera guy climbed out and approached. Jack Potter pushed the button at the door, spoke briefly, and then stood back.

Jon Haskill emerged from the building in less than a minute; the cameraman started rolling and Nikki switched her microphone on and extended it in Potter's direction. Potter put one hand on his revolver and displayed his badge with the other.

"Jon Haskill," he said, "I am arresting you on charges of arson and conspiracy to commit murder."

Haskill's face turned ashen and he looked, for a moment, as if he might melt into the pavement.

"Hold your hands out, please," said Potter.

Haskill looked puzzled and then understood; he extended his hands out, palms up, wrists exposed, and Potter handcuffed him. Potter and a companion guided Haskill to their car and into the back seat; Potter got in back with Haskill and the other detective drove away.

"Did we get it all?" asked Nikki.

"All of it," said the cameraman. "Not much, eh?"

"Oh, I wouldn't say that," said Stone. "It's the biggest story I've ever covered."

"Did you know the clinic was occupied when you threw the Molotov cocktails?"

Norman Brent dropped his head and shook it slowly.

"At that hour? Of course not. We figured the place would be empty; they didn't open their doors until nine o'clock in the morning. We figured, six o'clock, it'd be deserted."

"By 'we' I assume you mean you and Jon Haskill?"

Brent lifted his head and nodded emphatically.

"Jon, yes. It was all his idea. Our demonstrations weren't doing anything except annoying people. We stood out there for weeks and they just kept doing their dirty work inside. Nothing changed, babies kept getting killed. It wasn't right, it was sinful. He said we had to do something to stop them."

"Who suggested the Molotov cocktails?"

"That was Jon, too. Like I said, it was all him. Hell, he even gave me the bottles."

"We know that," said Emily. "He's being arrested right now."

"How? I mean, how did you know?"

"The bottles were easy. Did you know that every bottle CCC makes has a signature on it?"

"Huh?"

"On the bottom of every jar, every bottle they make, there are embossed letters. Pickle jars, olive jars, water bottles, they all have three Cs on the bottom. When we told the city's arson investigator about those signatures, all they had to do was dig through the debris from the fire until they found a shard of glass with a C on it."

"How'd you get that tape? I didn't even see a camera."

"Ah, that," said Emily. "That was just a bit of luck. The station where you bought the gas is just a block away from your apartment—Scott and I were there just a few days ago. I noticed it's a MidAm station and I knew they've been installing surveillance cameras in their stations. The company which installs the cameras also monitors them. They still had that tape of you when we asked for it."

"You asked for it?"

"That's the lucky part. The surveillance camera company is owned by my boss's son-in-law. They're called Bad Guy Eyes, by the way. Pretty apt, wouldn't you say?"

Brent groaned.

"One more question, Mr. Brent."

"What?"

"Are you the person who tried to shoot me?"

Brent sagged in his chair, silent.

"You shot my husband, you know."

He lifted his eyes and Emily saw defeat in them.

"I'm not saying another word," said Norman Brent. "I've got to call a lawyer."

That night, WSMP Team 8 devoted all its coverage to the bombing and the arrests. They amplified on it over the next several days. Carmen Howorth and Alicia Good joined the anchor team at the desk for interviews about their new facility and the new sense of calm and security they would bring to their work now that the bombers had been apprehended. Sean Sheehan did a long interview with

Emily explaining the forensic work which had gone into the identification of the glass bottles which held the Molotov cocktails. Nikki Stone's post-arrest interview with Detective Jack Potter aired several times. So did the moment which Scott Kern shot in the conference room after Emily's interview with Norman Brent.

"Mr. Brent," said K.B. Constantine, "I am a Chicago police officer on leave from the department. It is my duty to arrest you for arson, conspiracy to commit murder and the murder of Dr. Joan Estrada."

Her arrest of Norman Brent drew immediate attention from the brass at Chicago PD. K.B. was quickly assigned to a new station house where she assumed full duties; her complaint of harassment was resolved when the patrol cops responsible apologized; most assumed they did so under considerable duress from above. In her new house, K.B. was welcomed by most and two patrolmen asked the desk sergeant if they could be partnered with her. Both told her that she appeared to be on a fast track to better assignments and they hoped to catch that wind. In a few days, Jack Potter ran into K.B. and reported that the brass had moved so quickly and decisively because they'd been told that they'd be the laughing stock of the city if they continued to hold a cop who had helped break a major case on the sidelines. That advice had come from Gary Easton, who offered it begrudgingly.

Chapter Twenty-Two

"Once again, ladies, we raise our glasses to salute one of our number. Here's to Emily Winter, investigative reporter, crime fighter, all around swell gal and charter member of the Rules Committee."

They all raised their glasses.

"Great work," said Lois Lipton. "You scooped us all again."

"To my bosses' utter dismay," said Mary Massey, "We had to scramble to get anything. I spent hours talking the cops into letting us copy the gas station tape."

"Same thing in our shop," said Lipton, "my editors were all over the place looking for angles and interviews. None of us got anything fresh, Emily—you and your protégé there had the whole story."

Nikki Stone smiled.

"She's not a protégée," said Emily, "she's a reporter in her own right."

"I'm trying," said Nikki, "but the truth is, I never would have been there for Haskill's arrest if Emily hadn't shared what she had with Jack Potter. She's the one, had Presley send me to the parking lot. Emily had the whole story. All I had to do was show up."

"Not true," said Emily. "You're the one who tricked Brent. You got him to come to our shop—if he'd said 'No,' I'm not sure what we would have done."

Stone grinned. "Yeah, but that little white lie was all your idea."

"Don't forget me," said Linda Marshall.

"I haven't," said Emily. "I was just about to say, Linda's file on Chicago Container tipped me off. I never would have guessed they ID all their products if you hadn't given me that file with their whole history in it."

"We've got a problem," said Becca Bloomfield. "What?"

"Tradition says we buy drinks when one of us puts another crack in the ceiling, right?"

"Right."

"So does that mean we're buying for Emily and Nikki and Linda, too? My salary's okay—it's still not what the guys make, of course—but the way this crowd knocks 'em back, I could be broke before the night's over."

"You can count me out," said Emily.

"Why? You're the big star here."

"It's great of y'all to think so, but it doesn't matter."

"How come?"

"Benjamin just walked in. So did Greg and Alicia. I suspect they've made dinner plans. This one's my last drink of the evening."

"Not acceptable," said Bloomfield, "We have so much to celebrate."

"It's okay," said Emily. "We can catch up next week."

"I agree with Becca," said Mary Massey. "This evening shouldn't end before you get your due—we're all in this together, after all. You can't let us down."

"Besides," said Lois, "Alicia's been with us before, so she's already on the Committee."

"But," said Emily, "the guys—"

Linda Marshall jumped in.

"The guys can be honorary members for one night, can't they?"

"Wouldn't that break the rules?"

"How can we break the rules if there aren't any?" said Marshall. "Somebody find a couple of extra chairs, we'll make a night of it."

They squeezed Alicia into the booth and found chairs for Ben and Greg. A new round of drinks appeared. Somebody ordered a platter of cold cuts and cheeses.

"I have a bit of news," said Alicia, "about the prosecution of Haskill and Brent."

"What?"

"I was in court today. Just a preliminary hearing which lasted about five minutes, but the halls were buzzing."

"About what?" asked Lipton.

"Those two are at war with one another. Haskill says that the bombing was all Brent's idea and all he did was contribute two large bottles. Brent says the plan to destroy the clinic was all Haskill."

Mary Massey laughed. "'Not me, your Honor! Hang the other guy.'"

"There's more," said Alicia. "Haskill insists that he had nothing to do with Brent taking shots at Emily. He says Brent was freelancing. Brent swears that's a lie."

"And in the meantime," said Lois Lipton, "my editor had me get in touch with Carol Lobes. He figured, she's the last one standing, so we wanted to find out what's going to happen with RTLC."

"That's good reporting," said Emily. She turned to Stone. "Why didn't we think of that?"

Stone said, "Offhand, I'd say we were kind of occupied with other stuff."

"So, what did Mrs. Lobes have to say?"

"She quit," said Lipton. "She told me she can't be part of an organization which claims to cherish all life while it takes one and tries to take another. She said her faith doesn't have room for anything other than absolute support of everyone's right to life. She also went out of her way to make sure we understood that she had nothing to do with what Haskill and Brent were up to."

"I believe that," said Emily. "She never had a leadership role. They just used her to do the grunt work."

"And to stand beside them so RTLC didn't look like a bunch of men telling women how to behave," said Lipton. "They used her."

"Men do that?" said Kirsten Bonner. "I'm shocked. Shocked!"

They all laughed.

"So what happens to RTLC?" said Bloomfield.

"Lobes doesn't know, doesn't care."

"It won't make a difference in the long run," said Alicia Good. "They won't go away, they'll keep coming at us. We're opening our new clinic in a few months and we fully expect them to be on our doorstep as soon as we do."

"Not on your doorstep," said Ben. "There are strictures in place."

"Exactly," said Greg Good. "The original injunction may need to be amended since the clinic is at a new address, but some form of the protections Ben won will certainly pertain at the new place."

"I agree," said Alicia. "I've already told our board that I'll be in court as soon as they show up."

"And I can safely predict that ACLU will be there to support you," said Greg.

"You won't defend RTLC's rights?" asked Massey.

"The injunction doesn't impinge on their ability to demonstrate," said Ben. "Their rights shall remain secure." He turned to Greg. "Should the question arise, my friend, kindly inform your colleagues that I shall not again argue on RTLC's behalf."

"What, you draw the line at defending people who shoot you?"

"A not unreasonable position to embrace," said Ben. "Would you care to see my scar?"

"Lord, no," said Greg.

———————

In their condo late that evening, Ben and Emily sat at the table in the dining area, each with a small cup of hot chocolate.

"I sense something amiss," said Ben.

"Do you?"

"I do. All evening at Riccardo's, you seemed a bit subdued, especially given the celebration taking place in your honor."

"Maybe I'm just tired?"

"Perhaps, but I sensed something more. You have every reason to be proud, but something was gnawing at you, distracting you. Am I wrong?"

"No, darling, you're not. You know me too well."

"I observe, I absorb, I evaluate. Does this have anything to do with your concerns about bias? Surely, you can't believe that your personal beliefs impaired your work."

"I could make that case. I had the facts right in front of me all along, didn't I? I know the Molotov cocktails were fueled by gasoline and I knew there were gas stations all over town with surveillance cams. I should have known, the minute I saw what Jon Haskill's business was, that he was an obvious source of the bottles."

"And you uncovered all that."

"Only at the last minute. If I'd been doing my job properly—being a reporter instead of being an advocate for NWCC—I would have put this story to bed in a couple of days."

"And on that basis, you are distressed? Honestly, m'love, you cannot berate yourself for delaying the ultimate outcome."

"You're right and I see that. I'm just saying, I could have been sharper if I hadn't been so determined to get those men. But it's not important, really. I've got a fix on the bias thing—I doubt there's a reporter in town who doesn't bring their own feelings and principles to most of what we cover. It comes with the territory, right? We're human. You've been right about that all along, Ben—the trick is to recognize the biases and keep them from getting in the way."

"So, that's not what's bothering you?"

"No, it isn't. I'll always be who I am and that includes my bias. As you have noted, as long as it doesn't make my work unfair, I'll be okay. I'll need to be careful, but I'll be okay."

"Then, what?"

Emily sipped her cocoa and stared out at the lake for several minutes.

"It's not how I do the work, Benjamin. It's the work itself."

"I don't understand."

"It is painful. It is agonizing. It hurts. I get the stories, sooner or later, but while I'm doing that, I live with them. When I'm chasing all over the place, sifting through fact and fiction, the reality of it becomes part of me. Dr. J is dead, Ben. That's a fact I don't just put in a story, I live with it, I mourn it, I suffer it."

"You cannot do otherwise, Emily. One of the most valuable facets of your work is the humanity you bring to every story you cover. That sets you apart—no, above—your peers."

"It's not just that a good woman was murdered, Ben, it's that there are people out there who murder good men and women. I live in a mean, ugly, violent world, Ben. I've spent years in that world and while I plow through it and do my job—"

"—as few others can."

"—perhaps. But while I'm plowing through it, I'm in it. I'm part of it and it's part of me. The horror of a Molotov cocktail, the violent destruction of a building devoted to good work, the massacre of a kind, caring wonderful woman, the pain and fear and anxiety visited on all the women who relied on the clinic—I let all of it into my life.

"I understand that I wouldn't be good at my job if I didn't absorb all that, but it wears on me, it eats at me. Do I want my life to be filled with all that ugliness? And what sort of life is that, in the end?"

"May I speak?"

"I was hoping you would. I'm feeling lost, Ben. I want your help."

"First, it may serve you well to step back and observe. There is no doubt that a significant part of your work is that horrid world you describe, but that world isn't your entire life. You have a wealth of good friends, you have a grand home in a grand city, you have Greg and Alicia and Uncle Max. And, I am delighted to report, you also have me. I'm here to hold you, to support you, to converse and confer and confide—I'm here to love you and that, ma'am, is not going to be sullied by anything in the ugly world outside."

"True," she said. "But, still—"

"Second," said Ben, "I wish to ask a simple question."

"What?"

"When was the last time you—no, we—when was the last time we took a vacation?"

"I don't know."

"Nor do I. That's undoubtedly because we haven't had one in at least three years."

"No, I guess we haven't."

"So, I propose that, tomorrow morning we consider possibilities. By week's end, we shall have made arrangements to vacate this city, my law firm, your work and all the unpleasantness which comes with it for no less than a fortnight, preferably three weeks or a month."

"Really?"

"No," said Ben, "not really. Absolutely."

"It would be good to get away. Someplace with a beach, maybe?"

"That would be wonderful. East or west?"

"East, I think. Let's go to New England."

"And so it shall be."

They sat in silence, tired, comfortable and content. They watched the occasional car move along Lake Shore Drive, the silhouetted trees in the park, the huge quiet lake beyond. The quiet engulfed them until Emily turned and held her husband's eyes.

"You do understand, I hope, that for all the trials and tribulations of my work, it is my work."

"Of course I do," said Ben, taking her hand.

"Good. Because, when we get back, I'm going to dive right back into it. I can't imagine doing anything else."

"Amen to that," said Ben, "our fair city would be far less just if you chose otherwise."

**Enjoy the books in the
Emily Winter Mystery Series**

Winter in Chicago
Winter Gets Hot

Available at www.open-bks.com,
Amazon, Barnes & Noble, and other retailers.